Tuscany

a novel

Tuscany - a novel
Published by The Conrad Press in the United Kingdom 2017

Tel: +44(0)1227 472 874
www.theconradpress.com
info@theconradpress.com

ISBN 978-1-911546-20-7

Book cover design and typesetting by:
Charlotte Mouncey, www.bookstyle.co.uk

The Conrad Press logo was designed by Maria Priestley.

Printed by Management Books 2000 Limited
36 Western Road
Oxford
OX1 4LG

Tuscany

a novel

Fay Henson

1

Five hundred euros

Oh, Mum and Dad are still in the kitchen I thought.

I'd just come down the stairs into the hall, where I could hear Dad speaking to Mum about something. It was just past eight in the morning and I'd thought they'd have finished breakfast by now. I was still wearing my pyjamas as my school had recently broken up for the summer holidays, so I wasn't in a rush to get dressed.

I turned the shiny door handle, and went into the kitchen which was full of the welcoming aromas of toast and percolated coffee.

'Morning, Mum, Dad,' I said. Dad was sitting at the wooden kitchen table in the middle of the room, holding open the *Bristol Post* local newspaper, and I could see that he'd finished eating his usual toast and marmalade; his plate held the crumbly remnants.

'Good morning,' Dad said.

It was a lovely sunny July morning and the French doors were open for a change. I went over to the worktop to put the kettle on to make the sweet mug of tea I looked forward to first thing; the kettle had just been boiled.

'Hi, Caylin, how did last night go by the way?' Mum asked while she wiped over the work tops. Before I could reply, Dad cut in:

'Can you please ask your friends to be a bit quieter when they drop you off next time. Someone seemed to rev the engine unnecessarily when they drove off, surely there's no need.'

'Yes...' I tried to respond.

'And really Caylin,' he added, 'don't you think it's high time you found yourself some friends who've got their feet on the ground, and who are more sensible?'

Dad usually found something to complain about when we met first thing in the morning, and sometimes I felt that he'd forgotten I was seventeen.

'Honestly Dad,' I said, 'I didn't think they'd made that much noise; I thought they were quiet.'

'Well they weren't, and it was difficult to get back to sleep,' he said.

'I'm sorry, Dad,' I replied. I made my mug of tea, then put it onto the table where I usually sat then went to the cupboard to take out the box of Honey Nut Cheerios, when the calendar caught my eye.

'What date are we going to Italy again?' I asked while I held the page up with one hand to look at August, and poured milk into my bowl with the other.

'Our flight's booked for the eighth of August,' Dad answered.

'Ah yes, it's written here; Bristol to Rome, zero six thirty hours,' I said. It was written in Dad's handwriting, and of course, typical of him that he wrote the time in his military style. I returned to the table to eat my cereal.

Some weeks ago, I'd thought: Finally, they'll let me stay home alone, *yes*. But then Mum went and said that if I went away with them, she'd give me five hundred euros spending money, *five hundred euros*. Well, you could imagine how I felt; forget the home parties and cleaning up after friends who'd drunk too much, I'd decided I was going. It only took me two seconds to accept after she'd said it, and it was only that long because I couldn't let any words out; I was in shock. Of course Dad had a bit of a moan and said to Mum that she'd bribed me to go, which I suppose she had really, but I remember she'd told him to shut up and he was to enjoy my company before I went to uni in just over a year.

I was probably staring into space when Dad accidentally knocked the newspaper supplement onto the floor which brought me back to reality. I watched him as he lowered his newspaper to pick it up and peered at me over his glasses. When he did that, just for an instant, I couldn't help feeling that my Dad was ancient, but he wasn't quite; he was fifty-two.

'You know, Caylin, it's a pity you don't go out with those friends from Clifton anymore, and what was his name...' Dad said but I couldn't stop myself from butting in.

'Come on Dad, I told you that we all fell out, and anyway, if you're meaning Matt, he's moved to London,' I said.

I was fed up with Dad's persistence in bringing up the group I used to hang around with including Matt, who I thought I'd got on with quite well, until *she* joined our group and diverted his attentions. Of course I was gutted when I woke up and realised they were going out together, but that was then. *Miss Push Up Bra* could keep him.

That group had ambition, Dad had said, yes that was true. It was also true that Matt went to London, but I'd accidentally on purpose forgotten to tell Dad that Matt had dumped me for a girl who flaunted herself like that. It was because Dad had quite liked Matt and I didn't want Dad to feel that he'd been deceived if he'd learnt that Matt had easily betrayed me for a girl who was far more willing to go further than I was. So the way I saw it, I didn't care if Dad considered him a good guy.

Apparently there were plenty more fish in the ocean, really; and how would we know if they were a good fish? I wasn't very happy with my life, and to top it all, next year I was expected to go to uni.

'London?' he said, 'well, at least he was intelligent enough to get into university, which is more than you can say about that lot you're hanging around with now.' As those words came out of Dad's mouth, I had to argue back. *That's it*, I thought.

'Oh come on Dad, that's not fair,' I said, 'and who said anything about university?'

'You know that I meet many types of youngsters and my instincts are usually pretty good,' he said but I interrupted him again.

'And how dare you criticise my friends, you really haven't a clue, Dad,' *think I'm taking a bit of a risk here speaking to him like this*, I thought. 'All right I know they're not like Bill Gates,' I said, 'but some have found themselves work since leaving school.'

Dad sat back in his chair while I defended my friends. I couldn't quite work out if he was looking at me in a stern or an intrigued kind of way, but he let me continue.

'There are a few who aren't so motivated,' I said, 'but at least they're good guys and we have loads of laughs *and* I'm happy when I'm with them.'

'I doubt they're that bad, John,' Mum joined in. 'It's too easy to criticise without really knowing what's what.' *Thanks Mum*. And Dad knew we were right; he buried his nose in the newspaper again. *Ha, I bet your darling soldiers aren't angels*, I thought.

With nothing more said on the subject, I finished my breakfast then put my things into the dishwasher and left the kitchen to return upstairs to the safety of my room, but I found it was just too difficult to stop myself from giving my bedroom door a very hard slam. I locked my door then sat on my bed right at the top and stuffed my pillow between me and the headboard, I pulled my knees up where I rested my chin. I really hoped I hadn't forfeited my five hundred euros.

I knew Dad loved me, he always told me - or mostly, anyway - when we all called out goodnight to each other. I also knew he wanted the best for me, but he really annoyed me at times. It was all because of the army why he was so bossy, and I bet it was embedded forever. He retired last year when troops were reduced in Afghanistan where he'd been a Major for some time. But he couldn't quite close the military book; he'd still travel over to Bath where he helped advise reserve soldiers at the TA centre.

It'd been a bit tough for all of us when I'd thought about it. For months at a time Dad was away with his sub-unit under a lot of pressure and with tons of responsibility and stress. We were always worrying about him, praying he'd return home safe and well. Thankfully he did of course.

It'd also been quite difficult for Mum and me to adjust as now he was back at home we weren't able to be as laid back like when he was away. I was sure he would have had a fit if he knew that Mum and me stayed up really late to watch horror films together. (And how strange it was to discover that a forty-eight-year-old could be just as terrified as I was; I'd always thought adults could cope with scary stuff.) Sometimes we got takeaway Indian meals or pizzas instead of cooking and then we didn't clear up 'til the next morning. It was kind of cool; Mum was kind of cool.

I looked across at my bookshelf that held my high school text books which made me feel anxious. I'd been more uptight than ever in the past days because I was worried I wasn't able to bring myself to tell Mum and Dad that I didn't want to go on to uni, that I'd truly, really had enough of studying.

I felt like my life had already been mapped out for me; Mum and Dad had scheduled in their brains that I was to continue with education. They said, to give me a good start in life, yes understood, but I'd had an idea that it was also to keep up with a swot of a cousin on my Dad's side who'd done *brilliantly*. Good luck to you, wonderful Tricia, I said to myself. Of course my parents wanted to be able to boast about me and I couldn't blame them for that. But it was my life; surely I could do what I wanted.

I was feeling sorry for myself. It was rubbish having a cousin who was excellent at everything, my Auntie Jan had always compared us, and so when I'd had an inkling she'd be visiting, I had tried to find a reason to keep out of the way. I hated her questions, and she'd even had the audacity to bring clothes for me which wonderful Tricia hadn't needed. I didn't want her clothes, I liked to choose my own. I knew it also grated on Mum's nerves too; well, she didn't exactly say it. She probably didn't want to offend, but I could tell how she felt. And anyway, even Mum had a bit of a laugh when we'd taken wonderful Tricia's things directly to Oxfam. I imagined a pretty African girl who tried her things on, and I hoped it gave her a lot of happiness.

I adjusted my position and stretched out my legs, that was much better. My feet stuck out from the ends of my pyjama bottoms; how ugly feet were, well mine anyway. I had knobbly ankles and my toe nails had chipped blue nail polish but much worse was that when I pulled up my trouser legs, I could see spiky leg hair. So that went on my *things to do before my holiday* list.

I started to think about a different list I kept in my mind. On that list I'd written that I wanted to be more independent and to be able to start earning my own money then, not three years later.

Actually, I had been earning a bit of money, just enough to spend on going out and buying the odd thing or two. Mum had found me a part-time job at her hairdressers, so I'd been going there every Saturday plus one late evening. I had to wash clients' hair and I'd done odd jobs for the stylist. But I hadn't liked it that much, especially when I had to touch gross, greasy hair and then forced to listen to the pathetic talk; most clients were born blabber-mouthed gossipers.

I was pretty certain my parents didn't have any particular money worries, even though they'd never discussed their money situ in front of me, but there'd never been much of fuss when I'd asked for some extra cash. I definitely knew though, that Mum had inherited our detached home here in Falcondale Drive from my grandparents who I believed had been fairly well off; something to do with buying and selling land years ago.

But how I wished I had my own place. I'd seen so many other guys with theirs. They were lucky to have their own space, and how lovely it would be to eat cereal straight out of the box or to be able to stay in my pyjamas all day if I wanted to. Heaven. I could even have cats. But all that seemed a million light years away, especially if I had to go to uni next year.

I wondered what Sora my Manga girl thought of me. I'd created her to look a bit like me with long auburn hair and big green eyes, but she was more beautiful than me. She was lucky her skin was perfectly clear and she didn't have freckles like me which became horribly noticeable when I'd caught the sun.

The sketches of Sora I'd finished in watercolour were pinned to my wall and I'd often wondered if she'd considered me frigid or maybe wise. I cringed when I looked back at a couple of times I'd been walked home by so-called boyfriends; Sora had watched us kiss and cuddle on my narrow single bed. I'd often been pretty close to giving up my virginity, but then I'd panic and put the brakes on. I hadn't quite convinced myself that boys weren't interested in *just that*, and so of course they hadn't any patience with me, and that was that. I came to the conclusion they must all be like it and so I was destined to ruin any chance of a good relationship; not that there would be one anyway.

I'd wondered too if sometimes, in my subconscious I'd worried what Dad would've done if he'd found out; if he would've gone berserk. Perhaps he would've flown round to the boy's home and hammered on the door, shouted things at him then made him run twenty times round the block. I could just imagine Dad doing that. Humiliation; wasn't that what Major's did?

Well anyway, it wouldn't be long before Dad could relax away from the military and enjoy the fine wines of Italy (his words) and Mum wouldn't have to do housework for a while. And me, I was looking forward to seeing Italy for the first time, *and* with five hundred euros in my purse, but I wasn't sure if I wanted to hang around with Mum and Dad for *two, whole, weeks*. The very thought of being stuck in a hotel filled with people their age and even older, had bothered me quite a bit.

My phone bleeped, someone's just sent me a message on WhatsApp.

Cay!! U awake yet? Have u remembered we'd arranged 2 meet Em in town? Let me know when u coming, Zoeeeee xx
Oh Flip.

Hi Zoe, course I am, yes I have and see you at yours in a few mins, Cay xx

2

Joe

It was the eighth of August.

'Ladies and gentleman,' the captain announced, 'we'll shortly start our descent to Fiumicino airport in Rome. Meanwhile, the crew and I would like to thank you for choosing to fly with us and I wish you a pleasant stay in sunny Italy. The local time in Rome is nine fifty in the morning.'

Dad stood up and reorganised the overhead locker and put Mum's holdall inside, and sat down again. I was sure he hadn't realised that I still had my bag with me; I'd tucked it under the seat in front of me where I could keep my eye on it. My spending money was inside it, an amazing wodge of twenty-euro notes and I wasn't prepared to let it out of my sight.

During our flight, I couldn't help noticing that a tall guy with short blond hair and an attractive profile, who could have been a bit older than me, was a fidget. It had to be at least three times he'd left his seat (the row opposite but the next one down) to go up in the direction of the loo then back again. But then he'd take far more time than it was necessary to turn himself away from looking in my direction before sitting down to face the front. The only people behind me were oldies, I supposed he could have been a weirdo; but there, we'd never find out.

I watched the cabin attendants rush along the aisle, the women with their bright red lipstick and perfect nails, clicking shut the lockers and checking us. I pushed my bag a little further out of view with my foot. For a brief moment, I imagined them at the end of their shifts returning home to their cats in their cosy flats or cute little homes and hunky boyfriends; lucky them.

Mum's never been keen on the landing part, she was holding my hand and Dad's. He was fine, he'd flown more times than you could imagine, including of course in many military aircraft. We were descending lower over long straight roads with tons of moving cars which looked like children's toys, huge buildings and massive car parks.

Everyone was quiet except for a couple of kids who whined; perhaps their ears had hurt. When I was younger my Mum used to give me a sweet to suck when we were landing. Everything was shuddering and I could see the back of the tall guy's head bobbing against the top of his seat which I found a bit amusing. Then we slowed right down ever so quickly and we stopped.

Inside the airport, the man in uniform who was sitting inside an open cubicle hardly glanced at our passports and waved us through without saying a word. He looked *that* miserable I wondered why he still wanted to work there. At least he was earning money.

'Is that what they call passport control here?' Dad asked. Dad knows a lot about security and slackness irritates him.

'Um, he was quite friendly though, don't you think?' Mum replied.

'Very funny Mum, come on, let's go now,' I said. I was eager to get outside and to see Italy.

'We need to find the holiday rep at the arrivals point,' Dad said.

We joined a lot of other people and followed signs to the exit and finally through the big doors into an area where people were being greeted. Oh yes, the kiss. I'd forgotten that the Italians greeted each other with a kiss on both cheeks. I liked that.

'Do you think that's her?' asked Mum. 'The woman over there is holding up something with an emblem which looks familiar.'

'Reckon so,' Dad said.

Mum was right, the emblem on the little flag had the inscription Deluxe Tuscany Tours. There were some people already standing near the slim woman, and probably as keen as I was to get going. It was as if she knew we were on her list; *was it that obvious?* I wondered. She probably looked at my pale legs sticking out from under my new swishy flowered skirt, covered in goose bumps after the horrible air conditioning. None of us had much of a tan, the sun in Britain was always so sporadic.

'Good morning, and your names are please?' she asked us.

'Wilmot,' Dad replied, his chest puffed out like a Silverback, 'John, Linda and Caylin.' I had to smile to myself as it was a wonder he hadn't clicked his heels together.

It seemed like we were a bit of a mix on this trip. Amongst us were two women, I'd thought aged thirty something, a well-fed bloke maybe in his forties, a stuck-up looking woman around that age (I didn't think they were together though) and two older women who looked like sisters. Wait, there were others arriving, quite a tall family; *and* the tall guy I recognised from our flight.

'Good morning and your name please?' she asked them.

'Morning,' I heard the man say, 'Thorpe, Edward, but you can call me Ted, this is Sandra, and our son Joe.' So that was his name. As the rep was ticking their names off her list, I inadvertently made eye contact with Joe. So stupid. That was the last thing I wanted to do, even if he wasn't a weirdo. I closed my eyes in disbelief. *I bet you're just the same as all the rest*, I thought. I must have made a sigh.

'Caylin love, are you OK?' Mum asked me.

'Yes Mum, I'm fine, just a bit tired from getting up so early, nothing to worry about.'

'Great, we're all here. Good morning, welcome to Italy, *buongiorno, benvenuti in Italia!* the pretty, black-haired rep said. 'My name is Nadia and I'll be accompanying you on the Deluxe Tuscany Tour over the next two weeks,' she said, 'I'm sure you all want to get to otel Rosaria so please come with me.' At this point Nadia slipped a pair of enormous black sunglasses down over her face and spun around, then she waltzed off through all the people. It must've looked comical when we all scuttled along behind her dragging our luggage trying to keep up.

'She doesn't hang about,' Mum said.

'You're right there,' I heard someone say behind.

We'd all managed to meet up again outside the terminal building. The sunlight blinded me, it was so bright. And that reminded me that I needed to buy myself some sunglasses. Then I remembered my money and checked my bag was still done up; it was.

We were led to a coach and a driver who was around Dad's age with a gigantic pasta belly and I doubted he'd ever done an assault course in his life.

'It's OK, love, sit by the window if you like,' Mum said.

'Thanks, Mum.'

It was true, I *was* quite tired and I wasn't really in the mood for chatting, so I put in my earphones to listen to my music and watch the world go by. I really hoped it wasn't going to be a long journey.

Occasionally I'd notice Nadia turn and speak to others, but I wasn't really bothered to listen. I think we'd joined a massive ring road which went all the way around the outside of Rome. I was amazed, our driver didn't seem to care about his speed, and

I was sure it would have been fast enough to scare the pants off any of my friends. And they weren't chickens either.

I watched the big scooters sweeping in and out close to the traffic, and cars swerving from one lane to another and many cut across in front of others to exit the ring road. And it was all at high speed. I had never experienced a motorway trip as awesome as that; Roman drivers were total maniacs and our driver didn't flinch once. You could forget the Almondsbury Interchange, this was dead cool.

My parents' reflections in the windows caught my eye. I could see Mum quite clearly, she was looking ahead, leaning a little I guessed so she could see through the gaps ahead between the headrests. I liked her dark brown hair, especially as it now reached her shoulders. She had a kind face, and this matched her personality, her dark eyes, rarely ever showed rage.

Dad's eyes were closed and his brow was relaxed, so it wasn't possible to see his expression what Mum and me called, his *officer look*. His black rimmed glasses were a bit skew-whiff, probably after he'd adjusted himself in his snooze. I took a sneaky pic of him, *couldn't resist that one, sorry Dad*, I thought. I sent it on a message to Mum and when it arrived, watched her reach for the phone and opened it. She laughed, and I thought she mouthed 'cheeky' to me. We were interrupted by Nadia's voice so I removed my earphones.

'*Allora*, we ave tirty minutes for to stretch our legs before we continue our short journey to otel Rosaria where a wonderful lunch is being prepared for you.' I loved the way she spoke English.

Our driver turned the coach into a parking area near a wood. We'd stopped close to a small town and I had to say that it was a relief to be able to get out of that tin can for a while. Some of the passengers did some stretching exercises as soon as they'd climbed down the steps, but I wasn't going

17

to show myself up doing anything like that. When I stepped down from the coach, I'd actually forgotten that it was hot outside as we'd been kept under a controlled temperature, as if we were delicate incubated creatures. We were born into a new world filled with warm wood-scented air and insect sounds resembling electricity pylons.

We were led by Nadia up into the old part of the tidy town of grey stone houses with green shutters and little shops. It was just like I'd seen in some magazines at the hairdressers, where you could have thought that the photo was make-believe and wouldn't really be so nice in real life. But, places like that actually did exist, I was standing in one. Someone was taking a picture of a cute tabby cat lying near some pots of bright red flowers; Mum said they were called geraniums. I'd wanted some like that for my cats to lie beside and so I added those to my *wanted list* too. Some of us stuck with Nadia and followed her through a curtain into a coffee bar. There was something really special about the sounds of clinking cups and the sight of chocolate cakes after we'd been travelling for hours and hours.

She spoke to the man like she knew him. I wondered if she'd been there with other travellers like us, last month, or even last week. That thought made me feel a bit *unspecial*; to think that we were only important to her or him just for that moment in time. I supposed that she'd be returning in two or three weeks with some more people like us and I'd be back in Bristol and back to worrying about my life. I forced myself to think about the present, and the fact that I was going to taste my first real cappuccino.

'Hi,' someone said behind me. I didn't really know who it was aimed at, and when I turned I was face to face with Joe.

'Hi,' I replied. I couldn't think of anything else to say.

'Nice cappuccino, isn't it?' he said.

'Yes, it's good.'

'I sometimes buy cappuccinos in Starbucks? How about you?' he asked me.

'Yes...' he didn't let me finish.

'But it's nothing like this, is it? This isn't watered-down and scalding.'

'Er, no,' I managed to get out. I was studying the brown leather necklace he was wearing which had a lovely small silver whale's tail.

'What design did he create with the cocoa powder on top of yours?'

I looked at my cappuccino, and actually, I couldn't even remember. I'd already destroyed the sweet brown pattern in the creamy froth.

'Um...' I felt utterly pathetic for not being able to respond; he was confusing me with his quick questions. Then I saw Mum turn round from the bar with the tart I'd picked.

'Excuse me, I must go,' I managed to say and I squeezed through a gap in between the others to reach my parents.

'Thanks, Mum.' I'd been saved by my Mum and a heavenly chocolate tart with pastry that melted in my mouth.

I hoped Joe was thinking he'd be wasting his time with me. I couldn't also help wondering if he'd wanted to test me to see if I could be a candidate for a holiday bonk and to have taken away his boredom of being with parents for two weeks.

And after that, I'd be dumped before we'd touched down in Bristol and I'd still be worried about my life *and* with the added bonus of feeling angered that I'd been used. But it would not have got that far anyway, I'd be dumped way before that when the brakes went on. Joe didn't look my type anyhow. But I wasn't even sure if I knew what my type was. I hadn't had a lot of luck finding out.

'*Allora*,' Nadia said, 'after you ave enjoyed your refreshments, there's something you must see before we leave. I'll be up in the small square on the right; come and see.' Then she was gone. I saw Joe leave with his parents and I tagged on behind mine.

It was the view.

'Wow, OMG,' I heard one of the women say.

'Shush,' her friend said, 'you sound like you're auditioning for one of those B movies.' When they were laughing loudly together I couldn't help laughing too.

'It's a bit different to Gloucester, innit?' I had to agree quietly with them on that. Those two seemed like they'd have fun together, which made me think it would've been nice to have had Zoe and Em with me.

Moving my phone around on camera mode, Joe came into view, and, I just did it, I took a photo of him. I hadn't a clue what I was thinking. Oh well, maybe the girls back home would appreciate a photo of him when I could get a connection.

'Hi, would you mind taking a shot of us with the abbey right behind?' I heard Dad say and saw him stick out his hand to greet the well-fed bloke with the camera.

'Yes sure, Carl by the way,' he said.

I stood between Mum and Dad for the photo.

'Thanks mate, name's John.'

'Anytime John.'

'Um, excuse me,' I butted in, 'I'd like one too with my phone, if that's OK?'

'Sure.'

The photos were nice actually, Mum had her arm around my waist looking really chuffed and Dad was standing tall as he always did.

We must've arrived at Hotel Rosaria around one thirty lunchtime, having been dropped off outside the reception at the end of a long gravel driveway. I wasn't interested in anything except food, I could've eaten a horse. I just wanted us to be able to drop our stuff somewhere so we could go and find lunch. We were waiting our turn to be checked in by the man or the woman in uniform behind the wooden reception desk, when I decided to pester Dad.

'Dad, can't we do this later?' I said, 'Oh please hurry up, I'm starving. I must've got on Dad's nerves, or maybe it was that he was hungry too.

'Look young lady, we have to complete these forms first,' he said '*then* we can have lunch.'

Point taken, so I sat down on one of a pair of black leather chairs and waited as patiently as I could and did a recky on the place. The big reception area seemed quite nice with white walls and some pictures and there were a couple of gigantic red ceramic pots with tall leafy plants of some kind. Quite often when guests brushed passed the plants it made the big leaves rustle together. Not far from me, some massive windows were open making a draft of warm air sending the long white curtains into a sequence which made me think of dove's wings.

I slipped off my ballet shoes and put my feet flat down onto the floor. I wanted to feel the marble to see if it was as cold as the marble I'd felt inside a hotel reception in Bangkok. It was, and I didn't care if anyone saw me; my sweaty feet were loving the sensation of being cool and free.

Finally, the man handed Dad some keys and was pointing to the right. I put on my shoes, grabbed my things and went with Mum and Dad to look for our rooms on the second floor.

I had room number eight, a little single room with a tiny bathroom right next to Mum and Dad's room. I originally thought I was going to have to stay in the same room as them, a double and single squeezed in together with hardly any room to move. But thankfully when Dad booked the trip, the rep found a single room for me. That was a massive relief 'cause I didn't think I would have been able to stick my parents snoring or anything else; if they did anything else anyway. Maybe they did still do it. I remember a friend said once that she too couldn't bear the thought of her parents having sex. It's all just too Freudian, I suppose.

I didn't want to waste anymore time in my room, I'd see it later and locked the door behind me using the strange flat key thing with number eight on it.

We went back down to the reception, and found some of the people in our group waiting with Nadia. She led us through the dining room to the terrace outside where there were a couple of long wooden tables ready prepared for us underneath white gazebos. It all looked so elegant.

'Sit where you want,' Nadia said, '*buon appetito*, enjoy your meal.'

Near to us was the well-fed bloke Carl, the two older women and the stuck-up looking woman. As soon as I saw someone else pick up some bread, I did the same; it had sprigs of rosemary and it was salty, but anything was going to be good how hungry I was feeling. I let a waiter pour a little red wine out for me, and I took a sip. It tasted a bit like berries, but it was really rich. I could have murdered half a lager it was that hot on the terrace and beads of perspiration were appearing above my lip.

'Go steady with that Caylin,' Dad said, 'it's fourteen percent, so best drink water too.' When we'd drank wine at home it'd never been fourteen percent, more like eleven, or even less because Mum liked the fizzy red Lambrusco.

From where I was sitting I could see Joe and his parents eating at the other table and I couldn't believe that he'd put himself facing in my direction. Surely, he could've sat on the other side opposite his parents. It was really hard not to look his way and I really didn't want to have eye contact with him and give him the wrong idea. I had no interest in him at all.

I was feeling stuffed after the pasta with tomato and garlic sauce, then some meat, then a tiramisu dessert. I really wanted to get up from the table but seeing as Nadia was there, I stayed put. My pencil case and sketchpad were packed in my luggage upstairs, but if I rightly remembered, there was a pencil inside my bag. I took a couple of white serviettes from a holder and began to entertain myself doing a bit of sketching.

'My goodness, you're really very good.' A woman's voice interrupted my thoughts. It was one of the older women.

'Thank you.'

'May I ask who the beautiful girl is?'

'Um, well, she's no one in particular, just a Manga girl.'

'Caylin's always sketching or painting,' Mum said, 'and if she'd had her way, her bedroom walls would be smothered in them.' Mum gave me a friendly wink.

'But what exactly is Manga, Caylin?' the woman asked me, 'I'm afraid I've never heard of it.'

'Um, well,' I said, 'Manga is a name given to a style of comics or cartoons originating in Japan some time ago; the comics have become quite popular now.'

'Your Manga girl is like you isn't she,' the woman said, 'does she have a name?' *Always questions*, I thought to myself.

'I call her Sora,' I said, 'which means sky in Japanese.' I got that in because I knew what would be the next question.

'I like that sketch in particular where Sora is holding a cat,' she said and pointed at one of the two I'd done.

'Really? You can have it, but it's only on a serviette.'

'It's lovely, thank you Caylin,' she said 'will you put your name on it for me?'

'Sure.'

The rest of the day was pretty dull; Mum and Dad were tired and didn't want to do anything in particular except hang around the hotel, and so after our evening meal, I said goodnight to them and went up to my room. First priority, shoes off, then I opened my window and switched on the TV for some company. Maybe if I searched the channels, I'd find a music channel or something. I managed to find a music video channel, it wasn't MTV but it was better than nothing even if I didn't understand a word of it. I plonked myself onto the little bed and sat at the top as I liked to, and stuffed the pillow behind me. Ha, there it was, on the back of the door next to some hotel regulation blurb; something written that looked like an Internet password.

It worked and I was connected; I wanted to speak to Zoe and Em and see what they were up to. Right then, Zoe was last seen on WhatsApp at twenty thirty-five, and Em at twenty-fifteen, and seeing they're an hour behind us, I should be able to catch them as here it's nine fifty.

Hey guys, at last I have Internet! How's things there? It's been a long day today, but the hotel is nice especially as I have my own room ☺. Thought you'd like some pics – this one is the French Alps we flew over, this one is yours truly with a cute cat, and this one is of a guy on our trip who's getting on my nerves, always staring (he's not my type, but thought you'd like him Em ☺ ☺ .) Hate to admit that I'm bored, probably shouldn't have come ☹ .Anyway, catch-up soon, OK? Cay xx

Hey Cay, he's sort of cute, and I don't mean the cat ☺. Sposed to be off out into town tonight with Zoe, but you know her, takes forever gettin ready. At this rate they won't let any more in! Great to hear from you, catch you later. PS don't be shy ☺☺ Em x

Cool pics! The guy doesn't look as crazy as I'd likem, but have 2 say he's got a nice bum!! What u waitin 4? Relax, go get some fun!!

Glad u ok though, and hope tomorrow is better 4u. Have to run, Em's gettin angry waitin 4me2 turn up. Speak again 2morrow, Ciaoooo Zoeeeee xx

I really missed Zoe and Em and wished that I was getting ready to go to the disco with them instead of being here.

3

Resentment

I think I must've passed out as soon as my head hit the pillow last night after all that travelling yesterday. Today was our first complete day here in Italy and I remember Mum saying that Nadia had organised for us to visit some old breed of pig called Cinta Senese on the side of a dormant volcano somewhere. Great fun; not.

It took us about an hour to reach the old volcano, I could see the big mountain looming boringly in the distance ahead as we were driven towards it. The sky was bright blue and ever so clear and felt like it was going to be hot again today but, of course, we just had to be going on the gloomy side of the volcano where the sun hadn't reached and it smelled of stinky damp.

I didn't really know what to make of men and women who wore exactly the same things. Wasn't Joe embarrassed? I wondered to myself. His parents were both wearing beige knee length shorts and khaki coloured vests, even their little rucksacks were twinned. They were a double act.

'I understand *che* here was a summer storm last night on *tis* side of the volcano,' Nadia said.

In places, there was quite a bit of mud. Well, we had two choices, either to go with it, or climb back into the coach and wait. The decision was made to take the plunge, that was everyone except me. Even the two older women wearing flat sandals were going.

'I can't go in that,' I said, 'I'll ruin these.'

I knew I'd be heartbroken if I marked my light green All Star shoes and I wasn't prepared to take the chance.

'Are you sure?' Mum asked.

'Absolutely.'

'But Caylin, why did you wear those?' Dad asked. I bet he was annoyed because he'd paid for me to see the pigs.

'*Allora,*' Nadia interrupted us, 'our driver Francesco will be waiting, so you won't be alone.'

'Don't worry, I said, 'I've got my music, I'll be fine.'

I watched the group pick their way across the dryer parts but just before they went round a woody bend, I caught sight of Joe looking back at me. I wished he'd stop that.

The wait was about an hour, during which time, I'd flicked through the driver's newspaper just to look at the pictures, climbed in and out of the coach a few times and listened to various radio channels and my music until something broke my boredom. Strange sounds were mingling with my music so I removed an earphone. There were shouts and some ridiculous high-pitched laughing, until it became horrifyingly clear.

I looked at our driver, his eyes practically catapulted themselves out of their sockets as we both watched the group return; most of them caked in mud. Maybe I shouldn't have laughed when I heard him say a few things I hadn't understood and when he did some hand gestures, but I was sure he wasn't happy to see them. After he'd flapped around for ages, those guilty were finally seated again on the coach, shoeless. His coach was his baby.

'So what happened that was so funny?' I asked mum.

'Apparently Nancy, the lady who likes your sketches, got her long skirt caught up in some bushes,' she said, 'but what they really found amusing was that everyone had seen her floral knickers.'

I closed my eyes in disbelief, embarrassed that some women didn't care about showing themselves up. I wondered what the driver thought about foreign visitors, because honestly, the older ones can be really childish.

'But Mum, those two women even had pig muck on their legs,' I said, 'promise me you won't get like them when you're older?'

'I'll do my best, but who knows; could be a lot of fun.' *Very funny,* I thought.

Why did old folks get like that, I mean what made them think they were cool when they'd reached sixty or something? I'd already seen too many video clips of oldies falling over at wedding reception parties because they couldn't hold each other upright, or when they'd thought they could ride a kids bike. Ha, and they tell *us* to act our age.

We were taken to a place around fifteen minutes away where we pulled up at a big stone farmhouse still somewhere on the side of the volcano and where we were going to be eating lunch. Some went to the loos to clean up and I followed Mum and Dad through the entrance into a cool open hall which had an ancient-looking stone staircase inside; our voices and footsteps echoed everywhere.

There were tons of sketches and pictures of fungi and plants all over the walls and when I took a peek into one of the rooms we were passing, some people wearing white coats were looking at what seemed like plant specimens. Their voices hummed inside that room like a bunch of bees. It felt like a strange place to end up for lunch and not what I'd quite expected. Perhaps it was a trick to get us there and use us for experiments, maybe testing which fungi was poisonous or not and we were forced to choose one to eat in Russian roulette style. The stupid thought of that scared me.

We continued to another room with more pictures and some long wooden tables. We were down to business; gorgeous cooking aromas were coming from a kitchen somewhere making my stomach beg for grub.

The men were putting themselves at the end of the table which was fine by me except I really hoped that Dad wouldn't divulge anything about me in front of Joe.

A man and woman kept coming in and out of the room with trays of different cured meats for us to try. Bit of a shame if you were a vegetarian in my opinion. My favourite dish was the pork cooked in a spicy sauce with beans and tomatoes and there was plenty of red wine, again. I wanted to say, *mine's a lager please*, but I wasn't sure if there was a choice. Everyone was drinking wine or boring water. From where I was sitting, I could see Dad was looking pleased with himself and living up to his word; I just wished I could enjoy myself as much as he was. Mum was happy too, which I was glad about, but when was I going to be able to spend some of my money?

Through lunch in that strange place, I spoke when I was spoken to and I made some sketches of Sora to relieve myself from all the excitement; if only. But then I just happened to catch what Nadia was saying.

'You'll love the trip tomorrow,' she said, 'the sheep's cheese making is interesting and you'll ave the opportunity to taste the different ones at *pranzo*, *scusa*, at lunch.'

Now that made me wonder just how many trips like those they'd arranged for us. I wasn't really worried about how the pigs were fed or how the cheese was made. I wanted to see city life, the shops, and people like me. I shouldn't have come. It was like my fears were coming true. I tried not to show my disappointment and fought really hard to hold back my tears.

From that moment, it was really difficult for me to act as if everything was fine and even concentrating on my sketches was becoming near on impossible. I was starting to feel trapped, just like I felt trapped in my home life and everything was planned perfectly for me and nothing I could have done about it.

I felt so angry; surely Mum knew that this type of holiday would not be up my street. And now it figured that she must've given me all that money to spend, if ever, just to get me to stay on holiday with them.

Looking back, I must have been blinded by the money. What I should've done was used my brain and actually asked Mum what the itinerary was going to be, then decided whether to have gone or not. I was regretting my decision and clearing up sick after a good night with Zoe and Em would have been the better choice.

I did my best to hide my resentment and as soon as we'd returned to the hotel, I made an excuse to go to my room. I just wanted to be alone for a while.

'Mum, I really need the bathroom and to have a bit of a rest, OK?'

'Of course my sweet,' she said, 'you feel all right?'

'Yup, just bursting and, you know, after the journey round those bends,' I said, 'they make me feel a bit strange, but I'll be fine.'

I closed my eyes and moved my right hand across my forehead as if I was trying to relieve my head, then I gave Mum and Dad a peck on their cheeks.

'Don't worry, I'm OK,' I said.

But I wasn't. I went over to the reception to get my room key and then I climbed up the couple of flights of stairs in twos, leaving Mum and Dad behind to chat to another couple. I couldn't help it, but I was feeling conned.

I fumbled with my flat room key thing to get inside; I definitely wasn't in the right mood to be sociable and just needed to hide away for a while. I undid my All Star's, frantically kicking them off and threw myself down onto the little bed, which for a split second noticed it had been neatly remade. I turned myself over and pressed my face into the white spongy pillow and cried.

I wondered what the time was and checked my phone. It said five fifty which meant I'd been asleep for ages during which time I'd managed to smudge my black mascara all over the pillow. I dragged myself off the bed and took the pillow case to the bathroom and gave it a bit of a scrub using shower gel and a nailbrush. Ta da, it came out. I stuck it near the open window to dry; couldn't see it'd take too long, what with this hot air. I wondered what Zoe and Em were up to.

Hy guys, it's me, how was last night then? Did you get in? Today we went to see some pigs (wow) then ate some! ☹ Actually it was scrummy. Know what? There's a woman on our trip, who looks really stuck-up, loves high heels but she can't hold her booze. I reckon one glass and she's zonked. ☺ Anyway, Mum put me in the picture earlier and she'd found out that the woman's a national magazine food writer, and, wait for this, there's a bloke on our trip who's hobby is photography and the stuck-up looking woman seems to hate him taking photos of what we've been eating, especially when he's gettin all serious with it. Well I haven't seen her get her camera out yet, she just gets really stroppy and struts around. Bit of a psycho if you ask me. You remember the guy in the photo? Well Dad said he can speak Italian, lucky him. Nothing much else to report, cept I'm still dying to see some life. I need your news!! Cay xx

'*A domani!* See you tomorrow!' Well that sounded like Nadia shouting. And it was. I hadn't realised until now that our rooms overlooked the front entrance. In fact, I could see Nadia inside her dirty Fiat Panda, waving her sun-tanned arm out of the window.

I felt really fed up. I didn't think I could stay on the tour another day; I needed to find life. Earlier, when we pulled into the hotel driveway, I was sure that I noticed a signpost somewhere near the turning which showed that the city of Siena was just forty something k's away. What was that in miles? I wondered. A bit less I supposed. That was it, decision made, I'll go to Siena. I felt myself go all hot and my heart raced, partly with worry on how my Mum and Dad would take it, and partly, but probably mainly if I was honest, excitement about leaving the tour to find something which could be much more fun. There had to be life in Siena.

But then the thought of Mum and her disappointment in me made me feel guilty about my idea, and consequently the thought of Dad being angry over Mum being upset, frightened me. What would Zoe and Em had done?

Help, I'm dead bored ☹ . *Tomorrow I'm supposed to go to a cheese farm, but I'm on the verge of legging it on my own to a city called Siena. If you were me, would you leave your parents until it's time to catch the plane home? I've got dosh. Please hurry and tell me what you think, I don't have long to get going or I'll get collared by Mum and Dad and it'll be too late. Hope you see this really soon. Cay xx*

Well, for the last fifteen minutes I'd been pacing around in my room trying to get together some essential things, like my five hundred euros, phone charger and plug adapter, toothbrush, make-up, change of clothes and underwear and at the same time, praying that Zoe or Em would see my WhatsApp message. But no such luck, the little ticks in the message hadn't turned blue which meant it hadn't been opened. Maybe they're both away from an Internet connection. I had really wanted to hear their approval; just needed to see the words *go for it.*

I couldn't wait any longer, soon Mum or Dad would knock on my door to see how I was feeling. Then I suddenly realised I should leave a note or something; It would have been so cruel to say nothing so I ripped a piece of blank paper from inside a book I'd found in the bedside table drawer. I daren't tell anyone it was a bible.

Dear Mum and Dad, firstly, I'm fine and you mustn't worry about me. I've decided to leave the hotel for a while and go to Siena; I'd like to see some city life and to find people my age. It's not far, I'll be all right. Don't worry, promise I'll contact you, love you both Caylin xxx

I couldn't think of anything else to put, my mind was racing and my writing was almost illegible I was *that* anxious. I grabbed my stuffed bag and closed my hotel room door behind me as quietly as I could. I stopped outside of my Mum and Dad's room and listened; they weren't inside. I slid my note under their door then went downstairs to the reception hoping I wouldn't be met by them along the way.

I handed over my room key, turned and walked towards the main doors. As the doors opened for me, I took a quick look through the windows to the terrace, and for a split second, thought I saw my Dad speaking with someone. My heart beat hard. *Keep going*, I told myself.

'Hey Caylin, where ya heading?' My stomach turned, it sounded like one of the younger women on our tour.

'We're going to the gym, why don't you come?'

'No thanks guys,' I said, 'catch you later.' And I just kept on walking; No way did I want to be held up.

I really couldn't believe what I was doing. My hesitant footsteps along the gravel driveway changed into a confident stride and I knew that I had a smile all over my face. It wouldn't have taken much for me to laugh out loud because I was free and finally heading somewhere I hoped would be far more interesting.

4

Aches and pains

It took me just over ten minutes to walk the long dusty gravelled driveway up to where it stopped and joined the main road. For the first time since walking away, I turned and looked back at Hotel Rosaria, and the moment Mum and Dad came into my mind, I felt an enormous guilt leaving them like that.

I love you both, and I'm sorry, I said to them as if they could hear me.

I had to force myself away from that spot because for a split second I thought it would have been better to turn around and go back. *Don't be stupid, you'll regret it,* I told myself.

The signpost with place names I'd previously seen was just along the side of the road so I went straight up to it. There it was pointing to the left, written in big white letters on a sky blue sign, Siena forty two kilometres. I checked the time on my phone, it was seven ten in the evening. I wondered if it would have been better to leave in the morning but it was way too late, I knew it'd be impossible to return. I had to get walking.

I didn't have a clue if it was legal or not to hitch-hike in Italy, but I didn't have much of a choice if I wanted to reach Siena before it was night-time, and I still had to find a place to sleep. I realised I needed to cross the road so that I'd be hitching on the right, the same side the traffic would pass, even though I knew it was safer to face the oncoming traffic which would be on the opposite side. I carefully crossed the road making sure I remembered to look firstly to the left.

Starting my walk, I stuck out my left arm and raised my thumb; *that's it then, I'm definitely leaving*, I said to myself. Plenty of cars, lorries and vans passed me, but not one stopped to offer me a lift, I was sure it would've been much easier hitching a lift back home. Some drivers even beeped their horns, but yet nobody stopped. The sun was still hot and occasionally little brownish-green lizards made me jump when they darted into the dry grasses right next to me.

Up ahead I could see some buildings, maybe there was a coffee bar or somewhere I could get a drink; I was dying of thirst and I was sure I could sense the beginning of a blister forming at the back of my right heel. Great. As I approached the buildings, it looked like the start of a small village and I was certain that further along on the other side I could see a couple of parasols. I hoped that those belonged to a coffee bar, and luckily they did.

From outside I could hear some people laughing and a radio was playing. *Should be OK*, I thought, and I went inside through the open door making a beeline for the bar. I didn't think they'd find room for anything extra in that bar; there were stands on the floor full of packets of crisps and the bar was filled with chocolates, a cabinet with a remaining sad and shrivelled croissant, and a few bowls of knick-knacks.

The barman who was pouring out a glass of red wine for an old man said something to me so I automatically smiled, even though I hadn't understood him and there was a barwoman who was taking some money from another man.

Behind her were rows and rows of lottery scratch cards and above was a TV showing lines of numbers. When the woman moved, I spied a Campari Soda clock on the wall which said seven fifty-five. My heart beat hard as I wondered what Mum and Dad were doing and if they were really angry.

The laughing I'd heard must've come from the three people sitting at a table I could see from the corner of my eye and they were near a slot machine which seemed to constantly flash and make annoying jingling sounds all to itself. Nobody else spoke to me, so I just waited at the bar feeling a bit useless, until the barman moved across to me and said something again I didn't catch.

'A Coca-Cola please,' I said. *Well, at least that wouldn't be so difficult for him; that drink is all over the world*, I thought.

He pointed behind me and so I took it that I had to go over to a tall drinks cabinet. I pulled the door open and got a lovely blast of cool air where I probably lingered a little too long before taking a can and closing the door again. I fancied sitting outside at a table under one of the emerald green beer parasols, so first I went to the bar to pay.

Up to then, I hadn't actually had to unravel my lovely wodge of bank notes and I found myself trying really hard to discreetly unroll it inside my bag. The rubber band flung off and all my notes unfolded and separated themselves. Fortunately, I didn't think anyone had seen what had happened, although I would have thought by that time, anyone had wondered what I was trying to do inside my bag.

I put a twenty-euro note onto a dish on top of the bar I'd seen someone else do, and smiled at him feeling awkward that it was a big denomination for a small can of drink. I think he forced a smile in return and didn't say a word to me when he replaced it with a ten and a five note and three euro coins.

Well I don't 'spose they'll mind, I thought to myself as I took a handful of nuts and crisps from the bowls which were left on the side of the bar, I guessed were there for anyone to take, but I purposely didn't make eye contact with the bar people in case it wasn't the thing to do.

I went outside and plonked myself down at one of the two tables and untied my All Stars and took them and my socks off as I needed to check out if I had a blister or not. Just great; a red, sore area was forming which definitely looked like a blister coming to me. I let my feet breath free for a while in the open air.

And also my left arm really ached from having held it outwards and my right shoulder hurt from continuously supporting my bag by the shoulder straps. Even my left thumb felt like it had seized up and didn't want to bend properly. I couldn't help myself from worrying because I knew that it was only the start.

Using my left hand, I managed to hold the ice-cold can and lifted the silver ring-pull with my right forefinger. It was really cold and fizzy and I reckon I downed half the can in one go.

The problem was, quite soon after I could feel a belch coming up and arriving at any moment, and then out it came. Very lady-like and how embarrassing. Then I thought about Mum and Dad and how disapproving they'd be if they were here with me.

I dug around in my bag to find my phone amongst all my stuff and the unravelled twenty-euro notes; found it. Both Mum and Dad had tried to call me. Well I hadn't heard my phone ringing, probably because of the traffic along the road. I'd also received some text messages too which I had better open.

What do you think you're doing, Caylin?! You should turn round and come back to the hotel right now. If that's difficult, let me know where you are and I'll get someone to come and pick you up. I don't know what's got into you! Dad

I supposed that text was only to be expected. I opened Mum's next.

Dear Caylin, I don't suppose you'd understand how worried we are about you, you're alone in a country you know little about, and what about the language? Please come back, we can do different things together, we can make it more fun. And PLEASE contact us as soon as poss. We love you very much Mum xxx

That one too.

I decided it was best not to call them because I was sure it'd be really difficult to get a word in edgeways and really, if I was honest, I was afraid they'd talk me into going back or I'd accidently let on where I was exactly, not that I really knew anyway.

Dear Mum and Dad, I know in your opinion it's wrong what I'm doing, but I'm 17 and perfectly capable of looking after myself. You must stop worrying about me, I'm fine and I'm happy. I want you to enjoy yourselves on the group outings, I'll write again soon. Love you too Caylin xxx

As I was putting my phone back into my bag, I heard another message arrive, but I chose not to look at it, not then anyway, I really had to get going again because it was already eight fifteen. I put my shoes back on, put my empty drinks can into a bin, and set off again in the direction of Siena with my left arm outstretched, only this time my bag was wedged under my arm hoping it would relieve my right shoulder for a while.

Just a few metres along the path, a big advertising board caught my eye making me stop to look at it. It was a huge colourful poster of what looked like a bareback horse race in Siena and a date of the sixteenth of August. I was feeling excited, I had to go to that event. No, *I was going* to that event. And seeing that big poster inspired me making me really want to get to Siena and be amongst the living.

My original thoughts were right: yes, the place I had been walking through *was* a small village. I passed a flower shop, newsagents, bank, and a mini supermarket; all so very quiet and not a person in sight. There were a couple of long side roads with rows of houses and I could see a church. That was it more or less, then I was out of the village and from that point, without a footpath to walk along. I couldn't wait to reach the city of Siena.

I noticed that there wasn't so much traffic passing either, not like before. *Come on, someone's got to stop soon,* I thought. I carried on walking along the side of the road and every time I heard a car or something coming from behind I stuck out my left thumb but I also had to make sure that I stepped in closer to the side so I didn't get hit. Why was it so difficult to hitch a lift here? I wondered.

The situation I was in was changing, and I didn't think for the better. It was getting dusky and every car passing had their headlights on. There weren't any street lights, of course because I was away from habitation, so all I could see were the occasional outside lights of villas or homes in the distance. Even the insects had traded places with those I'd heard earlier; so many different sounds. But what could I have done? I couldn't just sit on the side of this road and wait for the morning, I had to keep going.

Ouch, I called out, *Ouch that really, really hurt.* My poor ankle. I hadn't seen the stupid drain. I prayed it was only a twist and wasn't a sprain. I didn't know why, but I started to laugh, partly because it made my right foot feel all weak and funny, and partly because I couldn't believe what I'd just done. A total nightmare.

I stepped as gently as I could, trying not to put too much weight on my foot but then I began to have second thoughts; maybe it was best if I stood still, even sat down and hitched.

At that rate it felt like I was never going to reach Siena and I started to feel a bit sorry for myself, again.

I wasn't sure, but I thought I could see a junction up ahead. I decided that I should get as far as there at least before stopping. It seemed to be a good move, there was a bus stop of all things, although I didn't think I'd seen any buses, and even a low wall where I could sit and rest my ankle. I stuck my thumb out again.

Usual thing; the cars carried on going past me. I wondered what the time was and pulled out my phone, it was just before nine thirty and I was beginning to feel up the creek. There were three missed calls. I was tired, hungry, thirsty, sweaty and had painful places. And I still had to find somewhere to sleep. If I'd known it was going to be that difficult, I don't know if I would've bothered.

But finally and unbelievably a car had stopped just a few metres away and was reversing back towards me with its hazard lights flashing and pulling in next to me. *Here goes then*, I thought. I could hear some music and some voices. My heart beat hard as I went up to the passenger door. The window was already down and a bloke was sitting with his elbow on the window ledge with a stupid kind of grin on his face. The driver was another bloke who was leaning across to look at me, he was wearing a gold chain which was dangling from his neck and in the back was a girl who was staring at me. I couldn't see her very clearly; I couldn't even tell whether her hair was black or brown.

The driver asked me something in Italian, but I hadn't a clue what it meant.

'I'm English; you're going to Siena?' I said a bit nervously.

'OK, no problem, come, come,' the driver said.

All of a sudden, I found myself hesitating. Perhaps I'd forgotten that there weren't only sweet old ladies driving around in cars. No, three tough-looking Italians had stopped for me and I felt like I couldn't keep them waiting while I was trying to think of an excuse why I was thinking of not climbing into the car with them. That single moment of hesitation seemed to last forever and I wondered if they could tell. I wasn't sure which would've been the best decision; to stay alone in the dark probably all night, or to get in the car with them. I didn't think I had much of a choice and was afraid they'd take offence and do something horrible to me if I refused their kind offer.

'*Grazie*,' I managed to trawl up from somewhere whilst I opened the rear passenger door and climbed inside the car next to the girl who I felt was constantly staring at me. Almost immediately we were pulling away not giving me any time to strap myself in as I've always been used to. I dropped my bag onto the car floor to keep secure between my feet and fumbled for the seatbelt; not one of them was wearing one. *Stupid idiots*, I thought.

I was able to let my eyes wander around the car's interior, the model of car I hadn't noticed. The driver with the gold dangly chain had short hair and was wearing a dark T-shirt and I thought what appeared to be long shorts, was joking about something to the bloke next to him in the front passenger seat. He also had short hair and from where I was sitting could only see part of a T-shirt. I was afraid to turn my head to the left towards the girl next to me in case she was still staring at me, but just from the corner of my eye, I was sure she was wearing a pair of jeans with rips in them. That's all I could make out in the darkness.

The girl leant forward and said something to the driver and subsequently he turned up the radio's volume although I wouldn't have said that the foreign music I was hearing was great, but it was better than silence and at least it helped me relax a bit.

Inadvertently, I made eye contact with the driver in the rear-view mirror and I was sure he was smiling at me. Of course, I had to smile politely back at him before turning my attention out through the window next to me.

Next thing, I was taken a bit by surprise because the girl leant forward again saying something to him and at the same time whacking him really hard across his head with her hand. *Ha, OK, I understand,* I thought, *he's your boyfriend or something. You definitely needn't worry, he's all yours.* And I made sure I wasn't going to look at that mirror again, I wanted to get to Siena in one piece.

It looked as though we were driving through the outskirts of a large place which I was hoping would be Siena. I saw a building with large metal shutters over the windows that had a green illuminated sign with a blue flashing cross, maybe it was a pharmacy. Another sign showed that the time was ten twenty-five. I was feeling much more relaxed now that we were away from the dark rolling countryside and now passing brightly lit fuel stations, hotels and shops. *It just had to be,* I thought.

'Siena?' I asked cheerily.

'*Si*, Siena,' the driver answered.

What a relief to hear that. Well, they could have robbed me and left me somewhere way back long ago, but they didn't and finally I'd arrived. I could feel that smile across my face again.

5

The jealous kind

Captivated was how I felt. We were travelling through long narrow streets, I assumed were one-way as the cars I'd seen were parked facing the direction we were heading. And scooters, I didn't think I'd ever seen so many and all different types, parked neatly together in lines.

We were passing people who were sitting at tables and still eating outside small restaurants and there were loads of bars with people inside and out and music was playing. I longed to join them. I wound down my window a bit more; the air was really warm with wafts of delicious things coming from the Pizzerias. And best of all, there were groups of people like me; they were strolling around eating ice creams and some were just sitting and mucking around. I wanted to join them too.

We continued along, turning from one narrow street into another, all the streets lined both sides with tall buildings of ancient stone. A lot of these buildings had what looked like garage doors on the ground floor and others with shops, shut for the night. If I looked upwards out of the car window, I could see rows and rows of shuttered windows, and I was wondering what was behind them. And what was it with the flags? In every direction, in every street there were colourful flags attached to the buildings.

I couldn't wait to get out of the car and I leant forward so that the driver could hear me.

'Um, *grazie*,' I said, 'OK, here, *grazie*.' I hadn't a clue where they were heading; I wanted to stay near the main part where I'd seen there was life.

'Where you stay?', the driver asked me.

'It's OK,' I said, 'no problem.' I put up my hand as if I was stopping him.

The girl next to me, who I'd never looked in the face properly, leant forward again and seemed to be demanding answers to her questions from the driver. *Oh no, please*, I thought. If she didn't stop that, I was sure he'd crash into a wall or something the rate she was going on and on at him. *I really should get out of the car*, I thought. I was feeling kind of awkward not understanding the jargon going on between them.

With that, we pulled into a tiny parking area and the driver switched off the engine and we all opened the car doors and climbed out. There were more flags there too. It wasn't bothering me that I hadn't anywhere yet to sleep, I was just glad to have finally reached Siena. I picked up my bag and when I turned to say thank you, the girl was already marching up the way we'd come, stopping at a small wooden door along the row of tall buildings on the right. *Ah, so this is where you hang out then*, I thought. I watched her let herself inside.

'Come, sleep,' the driver said.

'Um, no, really,' I stuttered my reply.

'No problem,' added the other guy.

Well, perhaps they were good Italians, and if they weren't, they'd already missed a prime opportunity to do me over and abandon me, but they didn't. At least I'd have a roof over my head tonight, *and* I could rest my ankle; tomorrow I could go and check out the bed and breakfasts. The only thing that was niggling me slightly was the unfriendliness of the girl.

'Well, just tonight will be perfect, thank you,' I said, whether or not he could understand me; I had to say something.

'*Perfetto*,' the driver replied.

Trying very hard not to limp, I followed the two guys up the street, stopping briefly to look at a flag hanging from a lamp. That one had an orange and white pattern with blue around the edge and in the middle was a shield with a unicorn. *Fancy*, I thought. I went through the door left ajar into a small tiled hallway. There was nowhere else to go except up the stairs to an opened door of an apartment on the first floor.

'Come, come,' the driver said.

At the top of the stairs we went through the door that took us straight into a room which had a kitchen and lounge together. My immediate impression, I would have said was *very scruffy*. I didn't think anyone ever bothered to put their stuff away. But who was I to criticise, these people were being good to me. I remember once hearing a really cool phrase, *never bite the hand that feeds you*. Maybe I should have remembered that when I left Mum and Dad behind. I was feeling uneasy thinking about them again and although I was only with them that afternoon, it felt absolutely yonks ago.

The girl was in the kitchen area taking some glasses from a cupboard and it was then that I could see what she looked like. She wasn't that tall, had longish dark brown (not black) hair and brown eyes and I'd say she was younger than the blokes she was with, probably twenty-two or twenty-three; I guessed they were something like thirty. When our eyes met, she seemed to half-smile at me and so I half-smiled back at her.

I was dying to take my shoes off and I wanted to check out my blister and aching ankle, so I thought it'd be OK if I sat on one of the settees with the least things on it. But before I could sit down, I still had to move a newspaper, a couple of TV commanders, some keys, a plate and some clothes.

I untied the laces and took off my All Stars then peeled off my socks and put my feet flat to the bare cool floor. My ankle was a bit puffy, but I didn't think it was as bad as I'd expected; maybe after sleeping with it elevated off the floor tonight, it'd be better in the morning. Same for the blister; it should dry overnight. I was trying to be optimistic.

I happened still to be doubled over whilst prodding my ankle, my bum pressed into the settee and my top half pushed onto my knees when the driver came back into the room. He came over to the settee and pushed the stuff out of the way and sat down next to me, where he also studied my ankle.

'No problem,' he said and got up off the settee and I watched him go to the kitchen area. I saw him take something out of the fridge's ice compartment and brought a bag of frozen peas over to me.

'*Grazie*,' I said and I adjusted myself to a more comfortable position and raised my leg to rest my puffy ankle on a cushion with the floppy bag of peas resting on top. I didn't know how long I could put up with the pain of the super cold peas, but I was determined to get the puffiness down.

Oh no, I thought, *not again*. This time it sounded like the driver was telling the girl off whilst pointing at some glasses of lovely cold beer I could see on the worktop. In fact, I reckoned it might have been because she'd filled three glasses instead of four. I'd already seen the other guy go and take one and then he went back to a room with it off to the left, so the other two glasses remaining must have been intended accidently on purpose for the her and the driver. She was leaving me out and I was feeling awkward because not only I couldn't speak Italian and say that it really didn't matter, but also I didn't want to be the cause of fights between those two. I thought I heard him call her Lula.

I was deliberately looking towards the TV which had been turned on when I sensed someone was approaching me. Of course I turned myself round and right close up to my head was a glass of beer Lula was holding at arm's length. It wasn't difficult to see she'd been told to bring it to me; her smile was more like a scowl. *Look at that*, I thought, she had a simple tattoo on her forearm in the shape of a bracelet with something written like Vico. It could have been a name of a previous boyfriend or maybe it was the driver. Well anyway, even if it wasn't, I could still think of him as being Vico.

'*Grazie*, thanks very much,' I said to her.

She didn't say anything; so that was her choice. I watched her go back to the kitchen area to get her glass then she followed Vico to the other settee where she perched herself on the settee's arm next to him. It was quite sickly watching her really, to see her leaning on him like that with an arm round his shoulder playing with his gold chain and stroking his hair. Well I certainly wasn't going to be fighting with her over him, so she was wasting her time exaggerating their bond in front of me. I really wasn't interested.

The beer must have been chilling for years, but it was wicked. I couldn't stop myself from gulping half the glassful in one go; the fizziness hurting my nose and making my eyes water, but I pretended it was nothing. I reckoned that Vico and Lula must have been regular drinkers, and didn't care about letting it all out, but when I sensed I had a belch rising, I let it reach a certain point that I could just manage to suppress it. I couldn't quite let myself do it in front of them.

That made me think about Zoe and Em and how sometimes we'd really laugh at that kind of thing. Actually it took me back to a time once, when I remembered that we were trying to belch and talk at the same time like you hear boys do, but it was harder than we realised so we passed it off as boys stuff.

I'd had enough of the bag of peas on my ankle so I got off the settee and went over to the kitchen area to put the peas away and went to where I'd left my bag to get my phone. For a moment my heart thud because I thought I'd put it on the chair close to the kitchen table and I couldn't see it, but then I saw it hanging by the handles on a chair near the hall door where I must've put it.

I sat back down on the settee and put my leg up to rest again as I was determined to give it as much chance as possible to get better before I left in the morning. Lula was still overdoing it on demonstrating their togetherness in front of me which I guessed was entirely for my benefit. I wondered if perhaps he'd been unfaithful to her in the past, and she was making sure I knew he wasn't up for grabs. It made me feel a tiny bit sorry for her because he wasn't taking any notice of her at all and instead he was fixated to the game of football on the TV.

I let my phone search for an internet connection, and what luck, there were a couple of possible connections available, albeit unsecure. But the day had been incredibly long and to think that this morning I'd been to see some pigs, well I sort of went, and what with walking and hitching, if you could've seen me, I was struggling to keep my eyes open.

How really strange it was waking up in different place again. I laid still on the settee for a few moments whilst I went over some events of yesterday in my mind. I located my phone that I'd slept on, sat upright and checked the time. It was seven fifteen in the morning and I couldn't hear any sounds within this apartment but I could sense the busyness with scooters outside of the building down in the street below. I wondered where the others were, hoping they were still sleeping.

I really wanted to check WhatsApp and also to send a text message to Mum and Dad as I never got to it last night, but as I was really bursting for a wee I'd have to do it after I'd been to the bathroom. What a relief it was to find that my ankle didn't feel so tender and the puffiness wasn't looking as bad as it did last night. I was truly glad about that.

One of the bedroom doors was open a crack enticing me to take a sneaky peek inside the room. I could see Lula and Vico asleep together but not touching, their hair all dishevelled and a single sheet half-on half-off them both. That room was just as scruffy too. The other bedroom door was closed where I assumed the other bloke was sleeping. I was afraid to wake anyone up so I stepped as gently as I could to the bathroom and turned the lock behind me.

I hoped they wouldn't mind me taking a little bit of their toothpaste to clean my teeth, after which I rinsed my face off under some cold-running water. *Wait a minute*, I thought. *Wasn't that my No. 7 Boots make-up I could see in the cabinet? Flipping charming.*

When I turned off the tap, I wasn't sure, but I thought I could hear someone speaking. I stood still and held my breath straining really hard to listen. There was nothing except my beating heart and some passing traffic in the street below.

I knew it wasn't right not to flush the loo even though I'd only had a wee, but I didn't want to risk waking the sleeping beauties, and so I went back to the kitchen area to try to find the internet connection. I took a quick look through the little gap of their bedroom door again and nobody had moved. Didn't they need to get up to go to work? I wondered.

Having spent ages trying to find my stuff, including my All Stars which I eventually found outside on a dirty window ledge thick with pigeon poo, if I could get a connection, I wanted to see if Zoe and Em had replied to me yesterday as well as opening a text message which I think came from Mum in reply to mine.

Caylin, it's worrying for us to think of you going off alone. One day when you have your own family you'll understand exactly what our fears are. Listen, you can call us for anything, and I mean anything. Keep in touch my sweet and no matter what, keep safe. Mum xxx

Well after reading that message Mum had sent yesterday evening, it left me with a bit of a lump in my throat, especially as I hadn't bothered to try opening it.

I really hoped Zoe and Em had written to me on WhatsApp and given me their approval on what I'd done. *Yes*, there were three messages waiting for me; I held my breath as I opened the oldest.

Cayeee, well, if twas me I'd stay with my parents & learn all about the farmland & become a country girl (only joking ☺). Think u need2 leggit!! Hope this message gets 2u b4 your parents come banging on that there door. Let me know what ur up2, take care, Zoeeeee xx

What a relief to have received Zoe's thumbs up. Now Em.

Hey Cay, I don't know if you would have seen this message in time, our internet was down so I couldn't open yours for ages ☹. Anyway, I know what Zoe would tell you, and I think you'd guess she'd give you her blessing straight away seeing as she's more brave than I am. And so you're probably guessing what I think? Well, I don't think you should go alone, of course I want you to have some fun but you don't know Italy or the language. I'm really sorry Cay to be a party pooper this time, I think you should stay, and if you do, I'm sure things will liven up a bit more ☺. Whatever you do, keep in touch and stay well, Em x

I suppose I sort of expected that from Em; got her feet a bit more on the ground. I opened the last message which was from Zoe again.

KKK, 4got 2 say that we did manage to get in2 the disco, but only by a gnat's whatsit ☺, *the q was so long. Poor old Em was frantic as we had 2 run for the bus – my fault. Twas a good nite but a tad dif without u strutting your stuff on the floor* ☺. *Say ciao to Italy from me, Zoeeeee xx*

Zoe always made me laugh. I'd decided I'd reply to everyone when I felt a bit more relaxed and away from that Lula and her childish antics.

I took a piece of kitchen towel and found a pen amongst some junk on the side and wrote *Grazie and thank you for all your help*, then stuck it onto the fridge using one of their magnets hoping that Vico would see it; he was the kindest. At the top of the stairs, I pulled the apartment door shut behind me as gently as I could, and feeling relieved that our paths wouldn't ever be crossing again, I went down to the main door to the street.

6

Cold sweat

I pulled the external door shut and stepped out onto the narrow street. I was absolutely starving hungry and craving for a cappuccino and something to eat like a bacon butty; maybe there was a coffee bar up along here somewhere.

Now it was daylight I could see just how nice Siena looked and all the pretty window boxes filled with those bright red Geraniums. It must be great living here with everything on your doorstep; Vico and Lula were really lucky as I'd already walked past a takeaway pizza restaurant and some clothes shops.

Every now and again as I strolled along, I had to make sure I stepped in towards the side because of the white delivery vans which bombed along but they weren't as scary as the scooterists who'd zoom past and swerve round any person or object. And actually, the women were riding as dangerously as the men and nobody seemed to take any notice or shout at them telling them off; they were all obviously used to it here.

Some of the little doors that opened onto the street like the one I came out of had small rubbish bags left outside, so I also had to watch I didn't trip and hurt my ankle again; where were the paths? I wondered, I hadn't noticed any.

Just a few metres past the takeaway and clothes shops, as I'd hoped, I came across a coffee bar which was opposite a phone shop. Before I could enter though, me and a young woman, who'd propped her bicycle up against the wall, had to wait for a couple of business-type people to step outside and then we could go in to be enveloped in the gorgeous aromas of coffee. I really envied Vico and Lula for living right in the middle of Siena; whenever I needed to go anywhere back home, I had to catch a bus or scrounge a lift.

'*Buongiorno*,' I heard someone say. A girl behind the bar, possibly a bit older than me was waiting to serve me.

'*Bon jorno*,' I replied and feeling pretty amazed I'd said it. I didn't think for one minute I'd pronounced it the right way though.

'A cappuccino please, *grazie*.'

I had a quick look to see what other people were eating. Just cakes. She said something to me but I hadn't any idea what it was, so I sort of ignored it and went along the counter to look at what there was to eat. She put my cappuccino on top of the counter and followed me. I couldn't help feeling a bit disappointed as there weren't any bacon butties; just cakes.

'This one please.'

I pointed to one I chose that looked like a croissant which seemed to be what most people were eating. She held it inside a paper serviette and handed it to me over the counter just like that, without a plate, but when I looked, nobody had tea plates.

I wasn't feeling very switched on this morning, and instead of making life easier for myself and doing a couple of trips to a table I fancied sitting at, I struggled awkwardly holding my croissant, cappuccino and bag and feeling a tad pathetic. Then I thought I shouldn't have walked away without paying and went to stand up to go over, but the coffee bar assistant didn't appear worried about it; she was serving the woman I'd walked in with.

Having just about made myself comfortable at the table I was sure that I could see a WiFi notice near the bar so I went back to see; it sure was. I copied the code onto my phone and went back to my table and whilst I sipped my cappuccino chose to reply to Mum's message first.

Hi Mum, I'm sorry for not replying sooner, but everything is absolutely fine, I'm fine. I had a lift yesterday evening with some nice Italians all the way to Siena and I stayed overnight with them. They were all very kind to me, so please stop worrying about me. I've said goodbye to them now because I'd like to find a B&B. At the mo I'm sitting in a nice coffee bar with free WiFi, drinking a cappuccino and eating a croissant! Scrummy! ☺ *This coffee bar seems to like horses (tell Dad), there's photos of them everywhere with orange and white flags. Can't wait to explore. I'll write again soon, love you both, Caylin xxx*

I hoped that would put their minds at rest. The coffee bar was getting more and more busy, and another thing I noticed was that most of the people who came in, ordered an espresso of some sort and a croissant, scoffed it while standing at the bar, paid and went. I think if it were me going off to work, I'd still prefer to sit for a while instead of rushing it. I heard a message arrive.

Well hello Caylin at last! We're so pleased to hear you're OK and you've met some nice Italians already, that's good. However Caylin, we'd still prefer you to be with us. But I don't really think there's much hope of that! I'll try to relax, but never forget we're here if you need us OK? As you know we've got a trip arranged today to a place where they produce sheep's cheese, never tried it so looking forward to that, especially now I know you're happy up there in Siena. (Between you and I though, Dad's not been very easy to deal with because he's angry that you didn't return like he told you to. You know how he gets, anyway, hopefully they'll offer red wine with

*the cheese at lunchtime, and he'll calm down.) Got to go now to get
ready, we love you too, Mum xxx*

Poor Mum, well hopefully they'd enjoy their trip and maybe
forget about me for a while. I continued eating the croissant I'd
chosen and was taken by surprise when I bit into jam, apricot I
thought; nice, especially as I was expecting a plain one.

*Hey guys, I've only just been able to find internet again, but here I
am, safe and alive in sunny (hot) Siena ☺. Firstly though, thanks
Em for your message, I really appreciated your thoughts and your
care, but I think I'd regret staying with my parents, and don't
worry, I've been in touch with them. Anyway, to cut a long story
short, I hitched a lift to Siena with some Italians and ended up
staying at their place. They were sort of OK but I think the girl had
it in her head that I was interested in her boyfriend. I don't think
so, and if you saw him you'd agree with me too. Anyway, she was
dead jealous because he helped me ice my ankle I twisted (still a bit
puffy), and you'll never guess, this morning I found my make up
in their bathroom. The cheeky cow had been in my bag. Soon took
that back! Oh, and you know my All Stars, I found them covered
in pigeon s..t, 'cause someone (had to be her) had put them on the
filthy windowsill. ☹ Anyway, just so you can see who I'm speaking
about, take a look at the photo of her I'm sending next. Having a
cappuccino and croissant in a coffee bar for brekky (great start to
the day)and going in search for a B&B. Catch up soon, love Cay
xx PS., wish you were here!!*

I thought I'd probably been sat too long looking through
Facebook instead of getting amongst the people of Siena, so I
put my phone away and got out my purse. I knew that I had
a five euro note which will cover the cost for my croissant and
cappuccino, but I couldn't find it, nor the ten. I found the

twenties that I'd folded back together again and put away in one of the bag's zipped pockets with my phone charger, but that was it. So I took one of those with a promise to remind myself that I'd have a proper look a bit later; the five and ten must be in my bag there somewhere.

I went to the till and put the twenty on a little dish and waited for my change. The guy at the till knew exactly what I'd had; how they kept track on what every person ate or drank amazed me. He really quickly replaced the twenty with some change and a receipt, then served a man next to me; all done efficiently with a smile. I liked that bar and if I lived there, I'd go to that bar every day.

Back in Bristol I knew of some guys who wouldn't have gone back to the till and paid, they would have sneaked out and done a runner. That's something I couldn't do and anyway if I had, I was the type of person who'd bodge it up somehow and get caught. And then what? My dad would probably make *me* run round the block twenty times, send me into detention and I'd lose all of my privileges. My Dad could be scary.

Saying that, I reckoned that I've gone and blown it anyhow and it was very probable that he would already be planning my punishment for when I got back.

I'd strolled a few more metres after the coffee bar and noticed that interestingly, the flags along the buildings and above the shops were different now. Here, they were burgundy and in the middle there was an elephant with a tower, I was starting to become curious about the significance of them.

My ankle was beginning to ache and cheese me off as I could feel it becoming tight again which was worrying me a bit as I really didn't want to be hindered. Just up on my right past a stationery shop I could see there was a turning so I decided to go and look and see if there was somewhere I could sit down a while.

It led to a type of square, with a building in the middle; actually it was more like a long ancient roof with pillars holding it up in between other tall buildings. And most pleasingly, there were seats one of which I made a direct aim for. It was just great to be able to sit down in the shade and rest my bones, as my gran used to say.

There seemed to be more and more people milling around now, loads whizzing by on scooters and every available parking space was being taken within a really short time. To my right there was a large fancy building with pillars and arched windows and behind that, peeping out at the top was a very tall tower.

I got my phone out and checked the time although it wasn't that important as it wasn't like I had an appointment or something, except I supposed it was just a habit. *Gotta stop that,* I told myself, *after all you're on holiday.* Yes, that was absolutely true. I *was* on holiday. But I still couldn't stop myself from looking at the time though; it was already a quarter to ten.

Something was niggling me at the back of my mind. It was the money. The notes were definitely inside my bag and now I couldn't find them. Then it suddenly occurred to me; it *had* to be Lula even though I knew I'd no proof. *Weren't you brave enough to take the lot then?* I asked her as if she could hear me. I guessed she wasn't.

From where I was sitting, I could see shoppers and tourists going through an opening to the left of the fancy building and I wanted to see what was there so I got my things together and followed. The opening took me into another ancient narrow street filled with shops, and when I turned right, the street led into a humongous square with a sign Piazza del Campo. It was so open and bright, I was totally mesmerised at its hugeness, and the people, oodles of them sitting down on the ground.

It seemed like that was the thing to do; actually, there didn't seem to be much choice as I couldn't see any seats except for the ones outside of the coffee bars surrounding the square; the ones where you'd have to buy something, no doubt at a ridiculous price just because of where it was. It's like when you stop for a drink or something to eat at a nice hotel open to non-residents on a promenade or somewhere back home. I'd done that a couple of times in the past with Mum and Dad; you pay for the view. So I plonked myself down onto the brick patterned ground along with everyone else. I was more or less forced to face inwards because it slanted a bit downwards towards, which then I realised, what was the front of the fancy building and tower of which I was sitting behind only a few moments ago.

I loved seeing people like me, some sitting, some lying down in groups and chatting together. I wanted so much to be amongst them all. I was in awe of that place with the calm and happy atmosphere. There was no traffic which meant no noise, just a hum of voices all mingled with the chink of cups and saucers from the surrounding coffee bars. And it was all just a stone's throw away from where I stayed last night. A thought struck me; I supposed there was a danger that I could run into that Lula again seeing as she lived right in the heart of Siena. Anyway, I hoped I wouldn't.

And how amazingly easy it was to spot the foreign tourists; they were the ones who wore sunhats and carried small bottles of water wandering around and looking up at the buildings.

I was feeling quite chuffed with myself. I'd just got back from checking-out one of the streets nearby where I found a small English and Italian dictionary in a smart bookshop, the name on the bag was La Feltrinelli; I could have spent years in there, I spied a coffee bar with yummy stuff to eat (I planned on going inside the next time I passed) and I bought some cool sunglasses (weren't dear) from a man who was selling souvenirs from a hut over there.

And just to finish it off perfectly, I was sitting on the ground again in that incredible place with an ice cream and trying desperately to eat it as fast as it was melting. But that wasn't easy and I'd managed to drip a bit of the chocolate and melon onto my skirt.

'Hey, ouch!' I shouted. Someone had stamped on my left hand I had outstretched behind me to prop myself up, then immediately I felt a hand on my shoulder. I heard a girl's voice.

'*Oh mi scusi.*' A girl in blue denim shorts and a sleeveless top bent down beside me.

'It's OK, no problem.' I was massaging my fingers because really it did hurt.

The girl, who had massive dark sunglasses sitting on top of her head of dark brown wavy hair, could have been around eighteen or nineteen. She looked genuinely sorry.

'You English?' she asked me. I was starting to feel a bit hemmed in and embarrassed; the small group of girls she was with were stood towering above us. So I got myself up off the ground and she did the same.

'Er, yes, *si.*'

'My name is Stefania,' she said, 'and you are...?' I was impressed with her pronunciation. It seemed obvious she was wanting to practice speaking English, but that was OK by me because I yearned to make some friends.

'*Ciao* Stefania', I replied, 'pleased to meet you, my name's Caylin.' I smiled and wiped my sweaty right hand on my skirt then held my hand out to greet her. We briefly sort of shook hands and they sat down on the ground. *Now or never*, I thought.

'Can I?' I asked at the same time as I made an odd hand gesture towards the ground.

'Sure.'

I sat back down again, that time near the five girls who were all wearing silky deep red, green and gold coloured scarves, and all tied in the same way. I wondered what type of club they belonged to. I loved listening to them chatting and fooling around with their phones and occasionally I answered their questions. I was dead chuffed.

'You on holiday here alone?' asked Stefania.

'*Si* and no,' I said giving her a smile. 'My parents are in a hotel a few kilometres from here but I want to stay in Siena, so here I am.'

'Yes, Siena is a great place, bu this period of year can be crazy.'

'How old are you?'

'I have nineteen years, sorry for my English,' she said, 'I'm nineteen, and you?'

'Almost eighteen,' I said thinking that sounded better than seventeen, or eighteen next June.

'Where are you from, London?' another girl asked, 'I love London.'

'No, Bristol on the other side of England.' There was a brief silence because I didn't think they knew of Bristol.

'It's good there too, you know.'

'What's it famous for?' the other girl asked.

'Well, it's got an old bridge called the Clifton Suspension Bridge high up above a river, really cool shopping centres and loads of pubs and clubs plus a good football team.'

'Do you work or go to college?' I was interested to know about what they did.

'We attend university here,' Stefania said, 'we've just completed the first year, but in differen subjects.'

'My parents want me to go to university but I want to work,' I added drearily.

'What type of work?'

'I'm still deciding.'

'There are a lot of Erasmus foreign students at our universities,' said the other girl, 'they like it here.'

'What do you study?' I asked.

'I do natural and environment science,' Stefania said.

'And I do political science,' said the other girl.

'Wow, interesting.'

Smart girls then. I was wondering what Erasmus was all about and maybe when I was back in Bristol, I could find some information on it. If my parents insisted on uni, how cool would that be, going to a university abroad. I would put up with uni if that were the case. But then, thinking about it, perhaps it wouldn't be possible to study abroad any longer because of that Brexit thing.

Then my dream was lost, the girls got up off the ground and said *ciao* to me, all happy and having fun together. I got up too, straining not to show my disappointment. Maybe I could have followed them to see where else they hung out, and to find out about the coloured scarves, but then another thought came into my mind; what if they'd noticed my smudged pigeon-poo'd All Stars and it was that what they were really laughing about. I was so embarrassed.

Hey guys, an update – what you reckon then? Here's a pic taken from my window. OK, the photo's at an angle because I had to lean out a bit between the shutters, but at least you can see the street down below with shops and take-away pizza restaurants. Found this place half hour ago, they don't do breakfast just a dead basic room to sleep and a shared bathroom but I was lucky to find it as everywhere else I went to was full or totally expensive. This evening after I've sussed out the shower, I'm going a wandering, can't wait! ☺ Catch u later... Your news???

I was feeling great, I'd had a shower and changed into a pair of shorts and summer top and sandals; I was ready to experience my first proper evening in the centre of Siena. I moved the white lace curtain to one side so I could take a quick peek into the street down below; it was getting dark and there were still many people moving around. I pulled the shutters closed and opened the window inwards to let some air in before locking my door behind me.

As soon as I stepped outside into the street, the aromas from the pizzeria's ovens made my stomach rumble. I didn't quite know where to go for something to eat; it wasn't for the fact that I wouldn't find somewhere, just there was too much choice.

It was fantastic; I could do whatever I wanted without anyone giving me their opinion. How cool was that. I turned right and followed the pretty illuminated street, passing coffee bars open for aperitifs, restaurants and shops with people still browsing. I kept doing left and right turns into different streets which all looked exactly the same, and often I'd end up again back at the square, Piazza del Campo. But that was just fine; I was happy exploring, and to top it all, I discovered that Siena had a comic book store which I hoped would be filled with stuff about my favourite Manga characters.

And if I walked past window-shopping tourists, I pretended in my mind that I was Italian and I casually strolled around humming to myself like I had no cares in the world and as if I'd always lived there.

But this evening, the nice cosy mood I was in disappeared within an instant. I hadn't expected to bump into Vico, especially where he worked, although it was hardly surprising considering he lived so close, but it was his reaction to me that shocked me the most.

After I'd deciphered a menu on the window of a takeaway pizza restaurant, I peered inside through the door and immediately recognised Vico. He was working behind the counter. Wishing to be polite, I was just about to put my hand up and to say *ciao* whilst he was serving someone when I watched him slam his right fist down onto the counter at the same time as shouting something and staring straight at me. I felt utterly gobsmacked, and could tell that it wasn't very nice because the customers who were waiting to be served just glared at me. *What was it that I'd done?* I thought. *Surely he wasn't aiming that at me.* So when I turned to look behind me and discovered there wasn't anyone, I broke into a cold sweat and realised who the abuse was targeted at; yours truly.

7

New me

I was feeling a bit sick with fear from the menacing look Vico was giving me, so I immediately moved away and went up the street, telling myself not to look back. But I couldn't help it; I had to look back again to make sure he wasn't coming after me.

I could see him standing outside the takeaway pizza restaurant and shouting a word really loudly, something like *abro* or *ladro*. *What did that mean?* I wondered, and I couldn't, for the life of me, think of anything I'd done wrong. He really scared me. And just before I turned to continue up the street, I couldn't swear on it, but I was sure that someone who looked like Lula was standing next to him, smirking. I didn't think I'd ever felt so humiliated as that.

I tried painfully hard to keep a level head and to make it seem to the people around me that it really was nothing, I think I even pulled a face as if to question what it was all about. But if the truth was known, inside I was deeply upset. I needed to find someone friendly who could take my mind off it and whatever I'd supposed to have done.

My annoying ankle was starting to ache again, but I decided it'd be better if I went a bit further away from the people around that area before resting up a while. As luck must've been on my side, I came across a religious-type building which to my relief had steps I could sit down on. And there was a bonus too; I spied a bronze, well it looked like bronze, water fountain.

Having plonked myself down on a step, I took off my sandals and prodded my right foot, which seemed a bit puffy but nothing drastic, and waited for a couple of people to finish taking some mouthfuls of the running water from the fountain until it was my turn. I pressed and held the knob inwards, took some mouthfuls, then I held my ankle under the lush cold water for as long as my conscience would let me before stepping back to let others who were waiting. I sat back down again and let the warm evening air dry my foot.

I felt refreshed and calm enough to go and find another takeaway pizza restaurant. I could've stopped at an Indian or a Chinese restaurant I'd passed, but I didn't see the point in that when I could go anytime I liked in Bristol. I was craving for real pizza, not frozen and not deep pan.

It didn't take too long to find another place, but what took the longest was deciding which toppings I wanted. In the end and after I'd kept the assistant waiting for much too long really, I pointed at two big triangular slices, one with cheese and tomato and the other with added sausage.

It seemed to be quite a popular place with music coming from a radio and people of all types and ages going in and out picking up pizza and cans of drink from the fridges. And seeing as I'd never watched pizza being made, I grabbed a spare shiny red bar stool and sat with a perfect view of how it was done whilst I bit into my slices.

I didn't think I could ever do that job; the man never stopped flattening out the dough and spinning it around to make a circle then adding the toppings before sliding it into the red hot pizza oven. He was sweating a lot and every now and then I saw him take a swig of water from a bottle which you could tell was nicely chilled because it had condensation all around the outside. A thought occurred to me, I wondered whether he actually ate pizza or was he utterly fed up with the sight of it by then. I shuddered thinking about Vico and if he hated the sight of pizza too.

Some of the people buying pizza slices were wearing those scarves around their necks, and then it clicked; they were the same colours as what Stefania and her friends were wearing. And when I took a bit more notice of my surroundings, I saw the photos on the walls of horses and what appeared to be jockey caps in the same red, green and gold colours, with an image of a shield and a dragon. It was just like all the people belonged to clubs and they certainly seemed to love horses around there.

I felt I couldn't commandeer the stool any longer and left the takeaway continuing in the direction I was heading when I came across a noisy bunch of people, mostly teenagers who were sitting near or around some long wooden tables set within a tiny square. It seemed like they'd all been eating there, going by the amount of plastic plates and stuff, and again, they were all wearing those scarves in the same colours as I remember Stefania and her friends had worn.

Then I saw her. She was sitting on some steps outside one of the big ancient buildings with a couple of the girls I met earlier. I really wanted to join them, and to show them that I wasn't a scruffy person who always went around in pigeon poo'd All Stars and ice cream stains on my skirt. But I wasn't sure if it would be OK to just go on up to them. *Blow it, why not*, I thought, *what did I have to lose?* I could have done with some good company. So I took the plunge and went up to her.

'*Ciao* Stefania,' I said feeling a bit apprehensive.

'Caylin, *ciao*.'

Stefania put her hand out towards a space on a step.

'Please,' she said welcoming me.

'*Grazie*.'

'Stefania, can I ask you a question?'

'Sure,' she replied.

'Why do you all wear these?' I asked pointing to her scarf which was loosely tied around her shoulders.

'Is it a club?'

'*Si*, a type of,' she said, 'you see the gold and red flag with a dragon? this is our *contrada*, you can say it's like a club.'

'So you come here often?' I asked her.

'Sure, because here in Siena old town, there's always something for young people to do and so this is where you'll find us,' she said, 'this is where we like to meet up.'

Well it was especially good to know where she hangs out.

'Do you know the *Palio*?' she asked me.

'Er, no.' I didn't know anything about Siena and was feeling slightly ignorant.

'Our club will enter the famous Siena horse race against some other clubs of Siena...'

As Stefania continued speaking, I lost all concentration because I was sure that I caught sight of Lula who I saw gave me a strange smirk and went amongst some other people passing by. I tried to follow her with my eyes, but I couldn't see where she went. What was she doing there?

'Caylin?' Stefania's voice jolted me.

'Oh, I'm so sorry, I thought I saw someone I knew.'

'*Don* worry,' she said, ' you OK?'

'Er, yes, *si*, absolutely,' I fibbed.

'Stefania, is there a loo, sorry, I mean, toilet?'

'Sure, go inside, at the right.'

As I went inside the building, I had to squeeze past a lot of adults who were all talking and socialising together in this big hall type of place. To my left was a kitchen with stoves and loads of big aluminium cooking pots and trays where there were some women clearing up.

I found the one and only women's loo, and stood in a queue to wait my turn. Some women smiled at me even though they didn't know who I was and I wasn't wearing one of their club scarves. I rushed washing my hands under some cold water from a tap which I had to operate with a foot pedal but I didn't bother using the dryer so I could return to Stefania as soon as possible.

You'd never have believed just how happy I was being able to sit down in between Stefania and her friends and being amongst the gossip, even though I didn't understand a word of it; I couldn't wait to get back to them.

After I left the old-fashioned tiled loo area, I made my way back outside, only to see that Lula was speaking to Stefania, in fact they weren't actually chatting; instead Lula appeared to be telling her something and Stefania was listening intently. Surely they didn't know each other; that would've been too much of a coincidence. What exactly was she up to? I wondered.

When Lula saw me approaching, she turned and mingled with tourists passing by, and then I couldn't see where she went. It was so obvious that she had bad-mouthed me to Stefania because the moment I'd reached her, I was greeted with utter hostility from her and her friends.

'Caylin, don come here,' Stefania said using a tone I didn't like the sound of.

'But, why? what's wrong?'

'Because you are not welcome in this part of the old town'.

I couldn't believe I was hearing those words, I was totally confused.

'Do you know that girl?' I asked Stefania.

'This is not important, she said you are a *ladro*.'

Ladro; it sounded like the word I thought Vico was shouting at me in front of all those people.

'Wait,' I said, 'I don't understand.' I pulled out my new dictionary and flicked through the pages trying to keep my hands from shaking; I was worrying about what they were saying about me. Found it.

'Thief?' I was mortified. *The clever bitch*, I thought.

'And she said?'

'Said you take money from their house and you like her boyfriend.'

'That's not true,' I was almost shouting into Stefania's face in desperation. 'Why do you believe her and not me?' When I listened to myself, I realised I was actually pleading. I didn't know Stefania, but I'd instantly taken a liking to her and didn't want anything to get in the way.

'I'm sorry, we don want *un ladro* among us.' Then she turned her back on me, leaving me to feel ashamed and unwelcomed.

If there'd been stones lying around, I would've taken great pleasure in lobbing them at Lula. I put a hand on Stefania's shoulder where I felt her tense up.

'Stefania, she's the one who is lying,' I said, 'not me.' I knew that I sounded angry that time. But it was useless continuing; Stefania wasn't interested in me anymore, I was history and it was an understatement if I said that I hated that stupid jealous girl.

So I had no choice but to leave, and I *definitely* wasn't in any kind of mood to look around Siena anymore and just wanted to return to my room. But I couldn't concentrate in which direction I should take and the only way it was possible for me to find my room, was to keep track as to where the black and white marble tower of the Duomo was positioned because I remembered that it was situated a couple of rooftop rows away from where I was staying.

Back in my little room, I was so annoyed, I didn't feel like writing any messages and I also couldn't bear to look out of the small window to see people I could hear having fun outside in the street below. They weren't laughing at me, were they?, nah, that would be too bizarre. I was becoming paranoid and laid awake for ages trying to convince myself that tomorrow would be different.

A different day; not. When I opened the bedroom door to go for a shower this morning, there was a note stuck to my door saying, *ladro no welcome, no booking.* Just great; another kick in the teeth. I must've been followed by Lula and her calculating ways, spreading lies about me to everyone I was having contact with. But what really sucked was the part at the bottom of the note, *return painting or get police.*

What painting was he speaking of? Being branded a thief wasn't particularly funny, and now there was a threat about the police being called, I had to get out of there pretty smartish. So whilst I was sitting on the loo deliberating over what I should do, I came up with an idea.

Hey guys, lookee at me ☺ What do you think?

I sent Em and Zoe a selfie I took. I was dead chuffed. Must've caught the girls at the right time.

Cay, have you gone off your trolley? Have your parents seen it yet? What about your Dad!!! You look great and all that, but, why? Em x

No surprise on Em's reaction then, bless her.

OMG Cayeee!! black and goth, love it girl! Sooooo spiky 2. Get yaself some red lippy. Why? Zoeeeee xx PS got me thinkin bout doing it2, but don't tell Em ☺

Ciao Guys, ta for your replies. I've been having a bit of a prob with Lula I told you about, remember my make-up and All Stars? Well, she's a real psycho and I'm sure she's been following me and telling people who I've met that I'm a thief ☹ *Me a thief! U know I'd never steal, daren't. Anyway, this morning I had to leave the room I'd booked and now have to find somewhere else cause of her lies! Had enough of the mad bi... almost sure she won't recognise me now* ☺. *Not told Mum and Dad bout my hair (yikes!) Cay xx*

I was feeling heaps better knowing that Lula shouldn't recognise me and that she wouldn't be getting in my way any longer, and all I had to do was search for another place to stay and start again.

But the temptation of spending some of my lovely euros on clothes far outweighed looking for a place to stay, I'll just have to do that later. And what perfect timing, it was the period of the summer sales. Loads of clothes and shoe shops had massive signs in their windows showing prices with fifty percent discount. The girls back home would have loved it in those shops; I could just imagine them now, taking over the trying-on cubicles and mucking around. That made me a bit sad; it would have been great having them here and helping me choose some things to go with my new hairstyle.

How hot it was trying stuff on, and even though some shops had air-conditioning, I was still sweating like I don't know what, peeling my clothes on and off, and it was actually becoming more and more tiring. There was never enough room in some places, and sometimes I found myself trying to balance on one foot (not my right one) stepping into a skirt and then falling out through the curtain into the shop. Well, I was really pooped by lunchtime, but contented with what I'd found for the *new me*.

It was quite weird really, as soon as one o'clock came, the streets became oddly quiet, with a few people still wandering around the shops which stayed open during the strangely long lunch break. One thing, at least the coffee bars never closed. I knew that I was fairly close to the coffee bar I spotted yesterday, and after a couple of wrong turns, I found the triple-windowed place called Nannini and headed straight inside. The first thing that hit me was the scrummy display of cakes and stuffed rolls, the second, just how busy it was inside.

When I finished scoffing a type of bread, filled with delish tuna and even more delish tomato, all washed down with a cold orange juice, I went on a bit of a wander to find the loo. And that's when, just before I followed the sign to the loo leading down a stone spiral staircase, I happened to glance through a side window and saw some publicity outside on a board which immediately caught my eye. It was something to do with a comic book store which surely had to be the one I found last night and was a perfect reminder to go and pay it a visit.

8

My new tattoo

My first morning in another bed and breakfast and I thought I'd try out the shower. Why did anyone ever think that it was a good idea to have a shower without a cubicle or curtain, in the same room as the loo and basin? I asked myself.

I'd just spent ages trying to clear up the soapy and watery mess after my shower even though there was a little round drain in the middle of the bathroom where the water could go, but it was near-on impossible to stop all the shower spray going everywhere else. I really hoped that it would dry out before another person wanted to use it.

There were a couple of rooms on this floor which I was certain were occupied because quite late last night I'd heard some toing and froing between the rooms and the bathroom. I had to cringe to myself because they could have heard me practicing saying *arrivederci* in the shower.

When I returned to my room, I checked my phone and *voilà*, I'd a missed call from Mum who'd left a recorded message and there was also a text message too. I dried myself a bit more and rewrapped the towel around myself then sat on the edge of the bed in anticipation of opening the message first.

Hello Caylin love, how are you? We tried calling you a few mins ago just to see how you are. We hope you're OK and happy. I've also left a voice message we hope you can pick up. Where did you say you were staying? Love to hear from you very soon. Mum and Dad xxx

I'd better listen to the voice message.

Um, hi love, Mum and Dad here, sorry not very good making recordings. Have sent you a text message to check you're OK there in Siena. Where did you say you were staying? Did you happen to see any shooting stars? Apparently every year in this period there's the chance of seeing a lot passing over Italy, and last night a few of us laid on sun beds outside to watch out for them. Well it wasn't disappointing, I counted at least eight. The trip to see how the cheese is made was quite interesting, except your poor Dad has had to go to the loo more often than usual, something to do with the strong cheese he took a fancy to, and of course, mixed with the rich wine, well you can probably imagine. Anyway, he's a bit subdued this morning; said he'll probably skip the wine at dinner tonight. By the way...

It was good to hear Mum's voice even though she continued on quite a bit about various things. Twice she asked me where I was staying, and actually thinking about it, even if I wanted to give the actual address, I hadn't a clue what the street name was. Oops, poor Dad.

Hi Mum and Dad, I'm sorry I missed your call. Great to hear your voice Mum and sorry to hear about the strong cheese Dad; hope you made it back to the hotel room in time!! ☺ I'd liked to have seen some shooting stars too. You remember I said goodbye to those people I met recently, well I've found a nice room to stay in, and close to the city centre too. I can't remember the name of the street but it's steep and narrow! Great shops here Mum! Love Caylin xxx PS Dad, I'll let you know when I need some more money. ☺ Sorry Dad, just joking.

When I look at what I'd draped over the back of the room's single chair, maybe I did go a bit shopping crazy yesterday. I fell in love with so many things like the baggy cotton trousers with spirals, one black and white and another in orange and pink; really sixties, and strappy tops to wear over. Oh and a couple of long black gothy skirts which just about touched the ground.

One of the clothes shops I found was just like a boutique except it didn't have the fancy and expensive gear. Actually, I wouldn't have minded working in there; the woman behind the till was lucky. She had a brilliant view of that huge square where I first met Stefania, and she could whenever she wanted, look out through the single window and watch everything that was going on with the tons of people who were there again today.

And that was the shop where I spent much of my time falling in and out through the cubicle curtain and where I ended up getting most of my sales bargains.

I pulled open the small wardrobe door to check in the mirror if I looked OK because today I'd decided to go gothic for the first time ever in my life. It was like I could hide underneath the *new me*; it sort of gave me a confidence unlike I'd felt before. I even found myself doing a couple of poses and pouting my red lips as if I was on a photo shoot. *Hum, not bad*, I thought.

I remembered that the man said there was WiFi here, so time to suss it out before I went and got a late brekky somewhere.

Hey Cay, Em's asked me to include her on this message cause her internet's down at the mo. ☹ Guess who we spied yesterday?? Miss Push Up Bra, and, wait for it, a bit of a belly on her which didn't look like food had caused the swelling.....but b4u blame Matt baby, she was with some tother bloke with a full-on tan, shades, gelled hair, u no, u seen the type. Suits her down to the ground. Anyway, we hoped this would give u a bit of a smile ☺. How's things there? Seen any gorgeous hunks yet? Zoeeeee & Em xx

Yes, I did smile. It must've been her who dumped Matt, not the other way round because I remember he was totally mesmerised by her boobs. He would never had left her that was for sure, and another thing; I definitely didn't feel sorry for him. But thinking about girls and guys with babies; wouldn't that mean that she'd be able to claim and get a council home for nothing and they could all live together? I wondered whether that was their plan. I wanted my own home but as I wasn't particularly keen on children so it wasn't an option I'd consider.

Ciao girlies, wow, she's preggers! Would have loved to have seen those two strutting along together and he sounds right up her street too. It's a wonder how she'll cope when she gets all big ☺ *, and then there's the stretch marks LOL. Poor Matt; not. You remember I had to find another place to stay? Well once I'd pulled myself away from a comic book store, a girl in a tourist info place helped me find another room, luckily; as maybe I was leaving it a bit too late. (Wasn't all my fault 'cause the guys working in the store kept me talking, I reckon just so they could practice speaking English!) I just need something basic to keep the cost down as it's expensive to stay here. It's a bit like the other one with a shared bathroom and a little bedroom, but it's OK. No brekky again though* ☹*. Oh, nearly forgot, here's something to give you a bit of a smile too; Mum said that the food writer (remember?) had a glass of wine too many over lunch at the cheese making visit, and by the time they'd pulled-up at the hotel, she was out for the count. Apparently her face was squished against the window and wasn't a pretty sight from outside. Then even more embarrassing for her, was that she had to be carried to her hotel room* ☺ *. At this rate she's not going to get much writing done.*

Will send you a pic I took few mins ago, found some decent sales over here. What you doing tonight? Miss you guys, Cay xx

I closed the door and stepped down the stairs into the small hallway where I was immediately approached by the elderly owner.

'*Buongiorno,*' he said.

'*Bon jorno,*' I replied trying to imitate his pronunciation.

I had hoped that he didn't want to see me for any particular reason and butterflies in my tummy were making me feel anxious wondering if Lula had been there too and he was going to ask me to leave. But he just gave me a nice smile which was such a relief to think that he was only probably monitoring who was coming and going. Unfortunately, I didn't know what else to say to him except *arrivederci* .

This morning I felt so comfortable with myself going off into the main part of the city and mingling among the locals and pretending that I'd always lived there. And I was loving the feel of my long black skirt swishing around my legs and every step I took, in turn I caught sight of a sandal with bright red painted toe nails.

I couldn't quite understand why, but this morning Siena seemed to have a different atmosphere; it wasn't a bad one, but I'd say it was more like frantic chaos. Everyone had to be careful going along the streets and we all had to make sure that we quickly stepped into a doorway if we heard one of those little trucks belting along. There were loads of them passing by with tons of dirt, and then I found out why. As I was approaching Piazza del Campo, which I decided was my favourite area, I could hear shouting and short whistles as well as sounds of banging, and when I turned the last corner, it wasn't quite what I'd expected.

What really struck me were the many men and boys who were working really hard in the square under the sun constructing barriers and stands, and laying the sandy dirt down like they were making some sort of track although it seemed a bit of a strange place to put one. Gone was the open space and tranquillity. Then it came to me. When I was hitching a lift to Siena I'd seen a poster along the way, I remember it was something about a bareback horse race. It had to be that.

It wasn't a lie if I said that some of the boys looked truly gorgeous in their dark sunglasses and working without T-shirts on making it *very* difficult for me not to look at their sweaty mahogany coloured bodies which were glistening in the sun as they moved. Even some of them had those silky colourful scarves. Cor, I just had to take a pic for the girls; well if I was really honest, for me too.

I held my phone in front of me and moved it round until I spotted a couple of the strong and muscular workers, and took the pic. Hum, I wasn't bad at pretending to take a shot of something else. In a way, it was a good job that Zoe wasn't here; she'd be wolf-whistling at them and pointing her finger at me as if it'd been me who'd whistled. I could just picture her doing that and embarrassing me. Some policemen were constantly moving people away from the entrances of the square which started to make me feel that I could've been a bit in the way and maybe it was best if I left because I probably looked pathetic standing there gawking at the workers.

My ankle was feeling quite strong this morning, so I thought I'd take a chance and explore a different area of the old town. But how tiring and annoying it was to constantly dodge the never ending stream of tourists and shoppers along the narrow streets, and then continuously apologising to those I'd collided with. There were so many groups of foreigners wearing earphones following their guide and just wandering along behind taking over the complete width of the street.

It was like I was the one who was forever walking in the wrong place, tripping over pushchairs which were transporting red-faced hot and angry toddlers, or dogs with tongues out and panting. Those poor dogs who probably believed they were heading for a nice walk were instead cheated on, and had no choice but to be tugged along by their owners. Couldn't they have been left at home? I wondered.

I had to get away from the main drag for a while and find somewhere less busy, so I turned down the nearest side street and followed along where it soon became much quieter. There wasn't much to see except tall buildings and garages and entrance doors, and then I saw a little notice which made me stop and go back to read it.

Stuck to the outside of a closed door was a colourful and pretty design with *tattoo* written above it. Oh how lovely it would be to have a tattoo of Sora. I knew Mum and Dad wouldn't agree with it, even though *dear* Dad has a small faded tattoo of an English flag on the nape of his neck, but maybe I could keep mine covered when they were around, so they'd never know. I wondered what it was like having one done as I didn't know a thing about tattoos, but I guessed it'd be OK, after all, loads of people have them. There was also a handwritten note. I took out my dictionary, *mercoledì e sabato*, that meant, Wednesday and Saturday. I had to think about what day it was today as I'd lost all track of time; today had to be Wednesday.

I could see that the shutters were open on the first floor, but it seemed all very quiet considering that the tattooist was working today; there were no voices or sounds of anything. I took a deep breath and pressed the door buzzer.

A noise like a window being opened made me look up to see a woman on the first floor peering downwards at me. It looked all the world to me like I'd woken her up because her short jet black hair was all dishevelled and you could see that her eye makeup was smudged, but I was sure it wasn't so early, it was getting towards lunchtime more than anything.

'Tattoo?' she said with a smoker's voice.

'Er, yes, *si*.'

That was it, nothing else. I watched as she reached her tattooed arm out to pull the window closed again and waited on the street for a good five minutes when the door clicked open which I supposed was my cue to enter. I stepped over the pigeon poo-splattered doorstep and went up the stairs to the first floor and tapped on the door ahead of me. Mum and Dad would've gone mental if they could see me going inside alone and back at home we're always being reminded of the dangers, but somehow I was choosing to ignore everything I'd been taught.

I heard the woman's husky voice so I turned the handle and opened the door to go inside a front room. The woman looked a bit younger than I originally thought, more like forty now that she'd brushed her hair and touched up her makeup. I wondered if she was the tattooist. She said something to me, but I didn't get it.

'I'm sorry, I'm English.'

She pointed to a dentist type of chair which was next to a sideboard jam-packed with and tools and loads of stuff. I obediently sat down and quickly rummaged around in my bag to search for a sketch of Sora I'd kept inside a zipped pocket, the one I'd drawn of just the top half of her. I held it next to the inside of my right wrist to show her where I'd like it to go.

She looked at it then put it down with all the other stuff. I wondered how many tattoos she usually did on a Wednesday or Saturday, in a month, or a year here actually in her front room. Anyway that didn't really matter, I guessed they could do tattoos anywhere they liked.

'How much?' I asked, feeling quite ignorant not trying to say it in Italian. She said something I assumed was the cost but also held her right hand up with four fingers. Did she mean forty euros? I wondered. I leant over and took a pen from the sideboard and wrote a four and a zero on the inside of my palm and showed her. She nodded. Well that seemed OK I guessed, having never known what the right cost was; I've heard that people pay loads of dosh for a tattoo, so maybe this would be good value for money.

I was feeling very apprehensive and trying to convince myself that my Mum and Dad wouldn't want to kill me; 'course they wouldn't, these days nearly everyone has them. Right then it was now or never because if I was to change my mind and leave, I didn't think I'd be able to plonk my bum in one of those chairs ever again. Decision made.

How easy it was to walk right in and get one off-the-cuff just like that. But I'd be lying if I said it didn't hurt; it did a lot and where I'd clenched my left hand so tightly, I think my nails had made permanent indents into my palm. Bet Zoe would like it and I bet she'd approve. As for Em, I wasn't so sure, but who knows, when she gets to see it she might think it was really cool too. But hey, look at Sora and how beautiful she is with her long auburn hair and green eyes looking back at me from underneath a piece of cling film. Now she'd be with me forever.

9

Humiliation

I was back again onto the little street and debating what to do next. If I looked towards the right, it led further away from the busy parts and if I looked left, I saw the occasional person passing along another street which crossed this one. I decided to go in that direction.

I was really pleased with my tattoo, and what was really cool was the fact that if I didn't want anyone to see it, I just held my arm down or turned my wrist towards my body. That should work perfectly with Mum and Dad. I stopped occasionally in front of a window and pretended as casually as possible, to look at stuff for sale, but really I was moving my right arm in different positions like running my hand through my short hair or holding my hand under my chin like I was thinking about something. It was then that you could see it, and oh how I loved it.

Fixed to a wall was a sign indicating there were some escalators further along somewhere, and although I'd already walked around a lot, I was intrigued to see where the escalators led to. Yup, there were definitely escalators alright. I walked inside the entrance and stepped onto the first moving escalator to be taken down the steep descent, passing advertising boards and big windows which looked out on backs of buildings, and the people who were heading upwards on the opposite escalators to the left of me. I did my best to keep my new tattoo on show to the world.

Often I had to move to one side to let those people in a hurry get past. I was just content with staying in one spot until I had to cross to the next escalator. All the while I was counting each escalator, number one, then number two, number three; Joe? *What are you doing here?* I thought. *That wasn't Joe from the hotel who was always staring at me, was it?* I span round and watched him being transported upwards on the opposite escalator. Perhaps it wasn't him, and anyway whoever it was had already gone out of sight and I had to remember to turn to face forwards so not to trip on the gap of flooring leading to the next escalator.

Having thought that I'd seen that Joe, I passed it off that I was somewhat mentally deranged from earlier seeing all those handsome boys, and so I continued descending and finally stepped off the last escalator, making the grand total, of eight.

It'd felt like I'd been taken to the bottom of the earth; except there was daylight and I'd arrived at a really busy area which included supermarkets, coffee bars, places to eat filled with young people eating and chatting, and a sports shop. I followed some people who were hurrying through some huge glass doors and going outside to a spacious area. Should have guessed why so many people were hurrying around; the escalators also led to the train station.

It seemed just like every station I'd seen in other countries, busy, noisy, fumy, and the usual people sitting and staring with nothing in particular to do; the types we tried to avoid. And I could see a bike rack with some bikes secured by chains and padlocks, and one wheel which remained tied to a post, for which I guessed that the rest of the bike had been stolen. Wasn't it always like that at train stations?

I didn't need to be there and seeing it wasn't a place where I particularly wanted to be, I took the eight escalators back up to hectic Siena curiously wondering, where that Joe was heading. *Nah, it probably wasn't him anyway*, I thought.

Just how could I make some friends? I wondered. I found myself a step to plonk my bum onto so I could do a bit of thinking; I wanted to be sociable, so what could I do tonight? I wondered. Then a thought struck me; *of course, tonight I'd go back to the place where Stefania hangs out and see if I could find her. Maybe she'll be ready to believe that I wasn't a thief and we'd become friends again. It was so simple.*

Making that decision actually put me in a much brighter mood with anticipation about making up with her as well as showing her my new tattoo plus the excitement in choosing what I was going to wear. My goodness, what would she think about my hair? I hoped she'd like it.

I couldn't wait to go and find her this evening, but it still took me ages to sort myself out. First up, considering it'd be too awkward showering with the cling film over my tattoo I had to resort to a freshen-up at the bathroom sink. Then I'd spent ages going up and down the TV channels until I found a music video programme I liked, and which only played Italian stuff. It was surprising on how many English videos they showed on some of the channels and seeing as I'd already heard enough of them at home, for now I only wanted to hear Italian.

Then I messed around for ages trying to choose what I was going to wear to meet Stefania; I thought that maybe the orange and pink spiral baggy trousers could be a bit over the top for our get-together so it was best if I went for the black and white ones. Cor, listen to me, you'd think we'd already sorted everything out and it was all perfect, but in reality I was only kidding myself and I still had to face her for the first time since she shooed me away.

The air temperature this evening was lovely as I stepped out into the street and immediately into the flow of people strolling along. It seemed like nobody wanted to stay inside.

Little breezes of warm air rarely felt back in Bristol on a summer evening, flowed softly across my back and arms as I passed different street entrances. One of the entrances I passed where there were some young people sitting outside of a music bar, a nice waft surrounded me from that interesting and strange wacky backy smoke, and just for a few seconds reminded me of my home city.

I continued strolling along swinging my right arm back and forth and letting the air touch my bare tattoo, which I must say looked heaps smarter now that I'd peeled off the cling film.

Just before I reached the area where I hoped Stefania would be, I stopped because all of a sudden I felt extremely anxious. What if she publicly sent me away before I got a chance to explain my case or what if I managed to show myself up and botched the whole thing.

All I had to do was turn right at the corner next to the perfume shop and walk just a few metres to where her club was. It wasn't difficult to hear some music entwined with high spirited voices coming from that direction which sounded like heaps of fun and which I supposed Stefania was probably there with her friends.

Oh go on, I told myself, *after all you've nothing to lose.* But that wasn't entirely true, because if it turned out that I couldn't convince her that I wasn't a thief, then it'd be a dead cert that conciliation of our brief friendship would well and truly be off the cards.

On the other hand, if I turned and went away, I'd still feel there was a possibility that one day I could bump into her and things would work out OK between us. I hoped it'd be at least a bit before the time I had to return to my parents at the hotel, and in which case I could for the time being, continue to live in hope; hum, dilemma.

But why waste time? So I continued until I'd reached the area where her club was. The atmosphere rocked; how lucky they were to have a club so united and vivacious. Tonight seemed even more lively than when I was there the last time, and I thought she was bound to be part of the throng of people somewhere. My eyes scanned everywhere in search for her and her friends amongst all the young people. It was so difficult to find her amongst the men, women, boys, girls and even children who were partying and enjoying themselves. Very close by were a few boys, some beating out drum rhythms and some swishing large flags around in unison. I looked along the rows of people sitting at the tables where I was sure I saw one of Stefania's friends.

I continued to hover around the area feeling a bit out of place, playing with my phone for something to do while I decided on my next move. Stefania had to be there somewhere. People wearing those coloured scarves moved past me in small groups or in pairs and, and tourists still ambled past on an evening stroll.

It seemed absolutely ages that I'd hung around wasting my phone's battery, but it didn't matter because it was a good job I'd waited; Stefania was walking down the street towards me. So she hadn't been inside the building after all.

'Stefania, can we speak?' I asked refraining from grabbing her arm, 'please?' I rushed this at her as she reached where I was standing. She looked totally surprised.

'Caylin?' she stopped still and glowered at me.

'Look, I want to explain about that girl and her lies...' Stefania put her hand up in front of me, signalling me to stop.

'I don know what is with you and that girl, but I,' she paused, 'we, don want it ere.' My heart sank as I watched her move away from me.

'Please!' I demanded in a last ditch attempt. I couldn't let that Lula get the better of me. Stefania turned round and sighed.

'*Va bene*, OK I listen.'

I perked up and trotted along next to her not saying anything until she found two vacant chairs and pulled them away from a table and pointed for me to sit down.

'Thanks.' Stupidly, I hadn't actually thought about where I should begin.

'I stayed one night with that girl and her boyfriend after they had given me a lift in their car to Siena. From the very beginning she didn't speak to me, and I think she believed I liked her boyfriend, which certainly wasn't possible.' I tried to explain in the most basic way.

'Do you understand me, Stefania?'

'Yes, I think.'

'She did some things to annoy me, which included taking a few euros from my bag, I discovered later had been taken.' I continued fixing my eyes on her to make sure she was following.

'I did nothing to them, I just left,' I said, 'and I'm telling you the truth when I say I didn't steal *anything* from them, or from *anybody*.'

Stefania continued to hold a firm expression, so I kept on fighting my corner whilst she was still prepared to hear me out.

'You know,' I added, 'the girl also told lies to the man at the bed and breakfast, saying I'd stolen a painting from him, so I even had to leave that place.'

Stefania pulled a surprised look.

'I love Siena and I want to have fun here with people like you, not to steal,' I said, 'I really hope you'll believe me.'

'But why you change your hair?' Stefania insisted.

'Because I think that the girl is following me; I don't want her to find me and spoil my short time in Siena.'

'Spoil?' she asked, 'I don understand.'

'It means destroy.' But what I really wanted to say was muck-up with the letter *f*.

And finally it seemed that Stefania had got my drift as her expression relaxed.

'You want some pasta?'

Amen.

'That'll be fantastic, *grazie*.'

For the second time, I was sitting with Stefania and her friends and this time it was as a guest of the club. I'd never experienced an evening occasion such as this outside and I didn't know if I could've described the atmosphere.

Imagine the warm middle of August night air filled with lively chitchat and cooking aromas, where there were rows of people sitting at the long tables with party lights dangling from above, wolfing down plates of pasta and tomato, trays with pizza slices and trays of jam or chocolate tart, jugs of fizzy drinks, water and wine; all the while some were practicing beating the drums suspended round waists and others swooping flags from side to side.

I was gripped by the atmosphere; it was just as if I was a film extra, silently taking part in a scene which was happening all around me and being admired by the many tourists passing by. And that was one of those lush moments I never wanted to forget, so praying I had enough battery left, I got out my phone and held it high up in front of me and my new friends to capture that selfie, and there I was, smiling for England like my life counted on it.

'You wan to go to a pub?' asked Stefania, 'after we help here, we can go.'

'*Sì*, try stopping me.'

I tried not to show my eagerness to be with them, but it was kind of weird that all of a sudden, I was allowed to be part of their club again.

I followed Stefania, Erica, Sofia, Virginia and Olga through the stone walled entrance into the crowded wooden shack style of pub located in another street not far away from where we were. It wasn't anything like the pubs I was used to, the ones with angry-looking bouncers on the door and a charged atmosphere. This one was equally as rowdy, but came with a more welcoming feeling. We made our way past drinkers standing at the tall circular tables and waited our turn at the bar.

It seemed like most people were drinking either craft beers or a cocktail called 'Mojito', but what I really fancied was a beer or a lager and when it was my turn, I pointed at a pump which had a trendy pink label with *La9* inscribed, apparently meaning *the nine*, whatever that was meant to stand for. I handed over some coins and took my medium glassful. The evening was hot, I was hot and the beer was so refreshing, that I had to stop myself from gulping it back.

More and more people were coming in which meant we were having to shift around a bit to let them get to the bar. Stefania and the girls were often dishing out the Italian kiss on both cheeks to boys and girls they knew who came by.

I was surprised just how huge this pub was because from the outside it looked like an ordinary double-door entrance into a bar area, but then the pub tunnelled backwards and there were some steps which led up to some platforms where there were some tables and chairs.

The music coming from a few speakers was replaced by a guy's voice which sounded to me as a bit of an introduction, and then the atmosphere changed up to a different buzz level as a couple of DJs dished out some brilliant soulful house music. I was pulled along by the girls towards the end of the pub so we could be closer to the DJs. (Think I managed to say sorry for having bumped into people only three times.)

Some people were standing and trying to speak over the music and others were leaning over the balconies watching the rest of us dance. It was difficult not to dance with that type of rhythm and I bet that even if you weren't up for it, you'd have done it anyway.

But something didn't seem right when I watched a big bloke with a long goatee go up to Stefania and it looked as though he was speaking to her with a very serious expression. I saw her glance over to Olga who seemed to have her hand scrabbling around inside her bag as if she'd lost something. Erica was with her.

The big bloke nodded at Stefania and then they parted after she gave him a quick kiss, when I think he went back through the people towards the bar area. Stefania instead joined back in with the dancing again when I assumed it hadn't been much and everything seemed fine; then,

'We must talk, come with me,' Stefania said in my ear. *Oh,* I thought.

'Yes, *si.*' I wondered what it was that she needed to speak with me about and I couldn't help but worry.

I followed her to the loos. Thank goodness it was slightly quieter, at least I would be able to hear what she wanted to say. A couple of girls were chatting to each other as they were leaving the loo area, and as soon as they'd gone, Stefania broke the news to me.

'Olga's purse has gone,' she said staring straight at me as if she was waiting to see if I showed any signs of guilt. My stomach turned over.

'*What?*' I said, 'and you think it was me?'

'It strange you are here and now her money has gone,' she said with a scowl, 'that girl said you are a *ladro*.' I hated the tone of her voice and the way in which she was standing in front of me with her hands on her hips. I was starting to feel uneasy.

'Oh come on, Stefania, you really think it was me?' I retorted, 'and you'd rather believe that Lula than me?' *That's great*, I thought.

'Yes.'

'You've gotta be kidding me, I'd never steal from you.' How could it be made more plainly.

'I do not steal, I am not a thief.' I made sure I said each word slowly and clearly.

Next minute the entrance door to the loos flew open and smashed hard against the wall. In came Erica with another blow. She rushed out some words to Stefania which I couldn't make heads or tails of except I think I caught the name of Sofia. *Oh god*, I thought. Stefania came quite close up to me at the same time as I noticed Erica stand by the door as if guarding it. Wasn't she going to let anyone in, or out? I wondered. I didn't like how this was looking.

'Two purse gone,' she said. *What is it that's going on?* I thought.

'Well, I'm sorry, you'll have to get your facts straight before you start accusing me.'

My hackles were rising. I moved towards the door to leave, but Erica stood firmly in the way.

'I can't see the point in staying with you and your friends Stefania,' I said with a sharp voice, 'it's a shame you don't trust me, and instead you listen to that Lula. I'm leaving, so move out of the way please.'

Erica still didn't budge from the door. *What should I do?* I wondered. I've never liked confrontation of any kind, but now

I've found myself in a position which is forcing me to stick-up for myself, and which is something I've never been any good at.

'Give me your bag,' Stefania said holding her right arm out towards me.

'Nope, in your dreams.' *Stupid comment*, I thought.

'That girl told a friend that she see you take the two purse,' she said, 'I want to see your bag.'

'You mean Lula is here, in this pub?'

'My friend says she gone, but the girl said *you* are the ladro, give me your bag.' I tightened the squeeze on my bag under my arm.

'Sorry no, and don't you think it's strange that she's gone?' My voice increased its volume, 'don't you think it's obvious, can't you see it?'

What *was* obvious was that Stefania and Erica weren't going to be swayed.

'We call the police if you don give me your bag,' Erica piped in. *Great, that'll work*, I thought.

'Whoa,' I said, 'here, take it, have a really good look.' I definitely didn't want the police involved, and put in a cell or sent back to Bristol. That would be a big NO. To think of what Mum and Dad would do when they had to go and pay bail or what if they had to return to Bristol without me; the embarrassment I'd cause them.

I released my grip on the bag and tossed it directly at Erica seeing as she was the one who last spouted off.

'Go on, take a real good look,' I said trying really hard to hold back my angry tears.

I watched both of them go through my bag, all my little personal belongings, and after a long five minutes, everything was put back inside and Erica handed it back to me. Of course they didn't find any purses.

'OK,' Stefania said, 'you can go.'

'Thanks and don't worry, I'm happy to go.'

I pushed myself roughly against Erica still standing by the door where she sort of tumbled out of the way. I couldn't grab the handle quick enough to let myself out of the loos and hurry weaving through the happy pub-goers to get outside before I burst into tears.

10
Under orders

Someone caught hold of my left arm as I was rushing to leave. I spun round to see who was trying to stop me and was utterly taken aback to be faced to face with Joe, of all people. *So it WAS you who I saw on the escalators*, I thought. Instantly I pulled my arm away from his grip then wiped my hand in turn across my cheeks to rid the tears I knew had escaped. What a mess I must have looked.

'What's going on?' he asked me, 'You OK?'

'Er, yes, fine.' It was my turn to dig around in my bag except I wasn't searching for purses, just a tissue.

'Not true,' he replied studying my face. I'd forgotten just how tall he was, and just for a teensy moment, I imagined he could have been my boyfriend, and wanting to protect me, then I dispatched that thought as quick as it came.

'I don't really want to talk about it,' I said blowing my nose, 'anyway, what are you doing here, I mean actually here at *this* pub?'

'I don't really want to talk about it,' he replied with a pathetic grin. *Touché.*

'Actually, that wasn't fair, I'm sorry,' he said, 'this pub was recommended to me as the place where everyone hangs out.'

'Yeah I'll agree with you there,' I replied.

Joe looked across the street.

'Who's that big guy over there, the one with the long goatee?'

I turned and realised that Joe was referring to the bloke who I'd seen speak with Stefania inside the pub. It looked like he was watching us. It wouldn't be that he thinks me and Joe are in some kind of scheme together, would he?

'Oh, it's a long story,' I said, 'you'd be bored to death.'

'Try me.'

'Nope.'

It was too late, we should've walked away from the area, because now the bloke with the goatee was walking over to us. He came right up and looked at Joe straight in the eye and said a few words to him. There was a long sweaty silence between the three of us. I could see Joe was puzzling over some unfathomable words; really impossible for me to understand, except I caught the word *ladro*. I too so much wanted to understand everything and to be able to defend myself. And then Joe pulled a surprise on me.

Joe was speaking Italian and I was riveted to the spot. Of course, now I remember Dad mentioning that *lucky* Joe could speak the language. I listened trying to get the gist of it all whilst watching their expressions; one in particular I found annoying when Joe glared at me. Must've been the bit about the *ladro*. And then,

'Caylin, you didn't steal from the two girls, did you?'

'What would you think?', *now you're rubbing me up the wrong way*, I thought, 'course not,' I replied.

There was more discussion which I didn't take part in; shame because I would've loved to have known what Joe was saying about me. For all I knew he'd told him that I'd escaped from a loony bin and he'd been sent to track me down and take me back. Cor, I'd kill him.

'Come on,' he said, 'probably best if we went to another area.' *We?*

'Er, think I'll go back to my room thanks, I'm really tired.'

'Well, at least I could accompany you.' *Hum, please no.*

'I'm OK, really,' I said, 'you go on inside the pub, it's really good.' I tried to encourage him.

'No, I don't really feel like it now, perhaps I'll give it a shot tomorrow.'

Tomorrow? Seemed like he's going to hang around a while then. I pretended to yawn a couple of times.

'Night,' I said, 'catch up with you again sometime.' I didn't want to be rude, but I was edging away and he caught me up.

'Let me walk part of the way then.'

'OK, part of the way.' I couldn't be mean.

We walked along a couple of streets and I was feeling a little more relaxed away from the accusations.

'Hope you don't mind me asking,' he said, 'but why did you cut your hair, even change the colour?' And before I could open my mouth to respond,

'I mean, it's great and all that, but your auburn hair was stunning, unique.' *Oh for goodness' sake, stop that*, I thought.

'I can't divulge that information, I'm afraid,' I said, interrupting him. I wasn't sure if I really wanted to hear what else he was going to say. Silence came after that, so we both continued to stroll along.

'Hope you don't mind me asking,' I said, 'but how did you recognise me?

Joe stopped and turned to me with a bemused look,

'Recognise? Are you suggesting you wanted to actually change your identity?'

'Not exactly.'

'Does this mean that I have to ply you with lots of nice cold beer to get you to talk to me?' He was smiling. *Why should I have to reveal my stuff to you*? I thought.

'Nope, and I'm not keen on beer,' I replied, but this time I was smiling too. I quite liked his manner.

'That's not true either,' he said. *How do you know that?* I thought.

'Anyway, how *did* you notice it was me then?'

'Well, it wasn't that hard after I'd stopped to look inside the comic book store,' he said, 'at the hotel I'd seen you sketch at the table.' Then he took out a wallet from his back pocket and opened it up pulling out one of my sketches of Sora I'd done when I was bored. He looked a bit embarrassed that I then knew he'd picked it up and kept it, and I was stuck for something to say.

'You know, those guys working in there told me they'd been speaking to an English girl, and apparently *she'd* told them she was staying in Siena whilst her parents were somewhere else,' he said, 'so I took a guess they were speaking about you.'

'Don't tell me,' I said, 'they *even* described me, like my hair.' I was being sarcastic as I was assuming he'd been pumping them for information.

'They were the chatty sort, so I just let them carry on.'

Oh really, I thought.

Joe caught me glancing down at my tattoo.

'Wow, I didn't realise you had one of those.'

'I didn't have one,' I said rudely.

'Won't your parents be upset about you having a tattoo?'

'Dad's got one,' I replied while I admired Sora.

'It looks a bit puffy doesn't it?' he said. We both stopped under a light to look at my skin.

'Well, it's bound to be a bit, it's only the first day.' I shrugged it off hoping it was a normal reaction.

Joe sat down on a wall and beckoned for me to join him which I supposed wouldn't hurt, as long as he wasn't going to interrogate me.

'So you caught a train then seeing you were on the escalators,' I said, 'I didn't notice a station near the hotel.'

'No, no, I came to Siena on a bus and I got off somewhere near the station.'

'Oh.'

'Fancy a slice of pizza?'

'Er, OK, if they have one with wurstel,' I said, 'if not, margherita will be good, thanks.' Even though I'd already eaten earlier, I could probably fit something else in; anyway I was on holiday. I took some euro coins from my purse.

'Here you are.'

'No need,' he said ignoring my hand with the coins, 'I offered, back in a sec.'

I watched him walk with a confident stride across the little street to a small takeaway pizza restaurant. I hadn't taken much notice that he'd left his phone on top of his lightweight pullover which was draping over the wall, until that was, it notified an incoming message.

I knew I shouldn't do it, but it was just too tempting not to take a peek and see who was texting him at nearly midnight. Perhaps it was from a girlfriend, or his parents. I could see Joe standing next to the counter inside the takeaway and talking to the man serving him. Lucky him being able to speak the lingo. He turned and mouthed something through the window towards me which looked like he said he wasn't going to be long. I stuck up my thumb to indicate that was fine.

I didn't have long, so I double-checked he hadn't moved, then ran my finger down the screen to reveal part of the message without actually opening it. '*What?*' I said out loud. The words appeared in front of me, *John here, any news Joe? Have you found Caylin?* My dad. My dad had sent Joe to search me out and take me back to the hotel.

So, Joe had been spying on me, was that it? No wonder he wanted to walk me to where I was staying; just to find out

99

where I was, not the fact that he was interested in me. Oh no. I was feeling so angry that tears were starting to well-up, again.

I was torn between wanting to stay and wait for him to return so I could hear what he had to say, and wanting to walk away before he came back. But it was too late, he was coming. He'd better have a good explanation.

'Um,' I said, 'thanks.' I reached out and took the huge triangle shaped slice.

'Wurstel finished I'm afraid.'

'No worries,' I said, 'this is good anyway.'

I waited until we'd both finished eating before I came out with my opening line.

'How are my parents?'

'Fine,' he said shifting his position on the wall and picking his phone up. He wasn't looking at me, but I was watching him closely.

'Haven't you been in touch with them?' he said looking in another direction.

'Because you know how they are, seeing as you...' I stopped myself from continuing. He was then staring silently at his phone that he was turning over and over in the palm of one of his hands; he had a uneasy expression.

He slid his finger down the screen and clicked on the last unopened message.

'You saw this?'

'Some of it, I mean, I didn't open it.'

He stood up to face me.

'Caylin, you had no right,' he said sternly, telling me off like I was a child. I got up off the wall and glared at him.

'And you had no right to spy on me.'

It was just sooooo obvious it'd been his intention to search me out on behalf of my Dad and that the comic store had been the perfect place to get some info.

100

I didn't think he'd planned on an outcome like this, probably hadn't even thought what reaction he'd get if I'd discovered he'd been following me. Did he expect me to be over the moon he'd conformed to my Dad's orders? No.

'And for your information, I *have* been in touch with them, as a matter of fact,' I retaliated, 'anyway, I shouldn't have to explain myself to you.' Joe was staring at me with an annoying grown-up look on his face, as if he was waiting for the child to stop having a tantrum. If he'd grinned, I swear I would've walloped him.

'And another thing,' I was sure he raised his eyebrows, 'you can go back to the hotel and report to my parents now that you've seen I'm absolutely fine. You've carried out Dad's orders magnificently.'

'You finished?' *How dare he.*

'Yes, good night and *arrivederci.*' That was it, I was implying it was end of story, and now that I'd said it, I couldn't go back without looking like an idiot. So I marched away from him in a girly kind of strop, when I heard him begin to shout something out, so I slowed down a little still keeping my back towards him.

'By the way Miss Caylin,' *oh listen to you,* I thought, 'it was *me* who offered to check that you were really OK,' he called out behind me, 'your mother was upset thinking of you alone in a foreign city, I was..', he corrected himself, ' *am,* happy to come to see you.'

I slowed my step down to nearly nothing; did he really say he was happy to come to see me? I wanted to check that I'd heard him correctly, to be able to turn round and say, *sorry, but can you repeat that last bit?* But I wasn't brave enough. What if I only imagined he'd said it? I really didn't want to run the risk of looking even more stupid than I already did.

I turned round and waited for a group of kids to pass so I could see him again, standing a few meters away from me. He was straight faced.

'Look Joe, I'm sorry, I'm tired and I've a bit of a headache looming, I need to go to sleep, but I do appreciate that you volunteered to come here though,' I said, 'and thanks.'

Someone was closing a pair of shutters up above where he was standing making him look upwards where I caught a glimpse of that lovely silver whale tail pendant shining under the street wall light.

'Oh yes,' I added, 'I'll contact my parents in the morning to tell them I've seen you.'

I didn't hear if he replied as I didn't hang around long enough to listen, and walked in the direction of my accommodation.

'Wait,' he called out, 'I'll be outside of the florist shop near Piazza del Campo tomorrow evening at six o'clock if you're interested in meeting up to watch the horse race trials.'

'Bye Joe,' I called back to him.

Once I'd returned to my room, I went to the small window to close the shutter. Not everyone had gone to bed yet. There were still people going home and there was the occasional car driver trying to negotiate the turns at the ends of the narrow streets. It was a shame how the evening turned out with Stefania. I didn't think that she'd ever believe me again, so I guessed it would be pointless even attempting to persuade her. But I was very curious to find out what the flip that Lula was up to.

And as for Joe; when I think back to how I treated him tonight, I did seem to be a bit cruel, after all, apparently he *wanted* to come to find me.

I drank the remaining water from a plastic bottle in my bag and turned out the bedside table lamp. I was keeping my fingers crossed that the lingering headache had disappeared by the time I woke up in the morning. Should I have been with my parents, they would have already given me some paracetamol. Mum always kept some with her *just in case* she would say. I laid on my left side and dangled my sore right tattooed wrist over the edge of the bed; there was no way I could let even the sheets touch it.

11

Motherly hugs needed

I reached for my phone on the bedside table to check the time as I could hear voices and movement outside in the street. It was nine thirty. Something must have been going around because whatever it was I'd picked up, was making me feel terrible. I thought that after I'd slept, the headache would have gone, but hey, it was still there and I wasn't sure if I had a bit of a temperature too. I was going to have to buy some paracetamol as soon as possible, that was, if they sold it in Italy.

And what were all those bubbly-looking things on my tattoo? It all looked so ugly and red. What was happening to Sora? She seemed like a witch covered in warts; so monstrous. My poor wrist. I had to get out to find a supermarket which sold pain killers or anything to make me feel better.

I knocked on the bathroom door to check nobody was inside. In fact, it hadn't been long since someone had used it, the floor was soaking wet and the walls were running with condensation, and the stuffiness made me feel even more weird than I did already. Didn't they ever learn when they were a child how to open the window? I pushed it open, then just about managed to find the effort to clean my teeth before returning to my room, for which I then had the hassle of getting dressed.

I really couldn't be bothered to mess around getting ready and so I put on what I wore out last night. I even hurt when I brushed my hair; it felt like flu or something.

Well thankfully I was back in my room after tracking down a pharmacy. It wasn't as difficult as I thought in the end but that was only after I'd discovered that the small supermarkets didn't sell pain killers. I was lucky enough to find one after spotting the flashing blue and green sign hanging outside, the type which probably could have been seen from miles away, the neon was so bright.

When it was my turn to go to the counter inside the sterile and cold air-conditioned shop, I tried asking for paracetamol but the woman didn't understand me, so I wrote it down on a used receipt I found inside my bag. Apparently in Italy the spelling was almost the same except when she finally recognised it, she pronounced it really different to how I was expecting. She handed me a small packet called Tachipirina and pointed to the word paracetamolo, she'd taken from a cabinet behind her and zapped a scanner onto the barcode. As I didn't catch the cost for the third time, when she told me, I had to look at the till and if that wasn't a cure for feeling ill, I didn't know what would be. The price sucked.

In all, it took me around forty five minutes until I was back in my room with a packet of pain killers and a couple of bottles of natural water and within one minute of entering, I'd swallowed two tablets along with gallons of water. I pushed my sandals off my feet and climbed into bed with my clothes on and picked up my phone; I really had to make contact with Mum and Dad.

Hi Mum, Dad, thanks for your message yesterday which I've just opened now, but I guess you already know that I'm fine here in Siena, assuming that Joe from the hotel had reported back to you! Dad, did you ask him to come here and search me out? He said he volunteered. It's getting busier here now because I think they're preparing for some sort of horse race in the middle of the city, strange I know. Sorry to hear Dad that you'd run out of loo paper and you had to wait an hour before Mum returned to the room because she got side-tracked by someone downstairs. Aw Mum, that was really cruel ☺. Anyway, it was good to hear that you're finally able to go out again now. Love Caylin xxx PS Let me know about that Joe please. Love you lots xxx

That was all I could conjure up for Mum and Dad. I missed them such a lot. Mum would always give me a cuddle and do things for me if I wasn't feeling very well whereas Dad wasn't a cuddly type of person, but he'd always make me feel safe because he was still strong.

A huge wave of guilt engulfed me thinking about what I'd done to myself since being here in Siena mostly because of that Lula. I was sure Mum and Dad would be deeply upset and disappointed with me. How could they trust me after that? I was feeling so miserably low, I couldn't stop myself from sobbing into the pillow. Oh how I needed a hug.

Wow that was a weird sleep, all those strange dreams with Sora's face appearing everywhere. My phone's display showed that it was three thirty in the afternoon. Well at least I'd had a sleep and my head wasn't aching as much, but I was still feeling yucky and I was very sweaty. I gulped down some more water. I laid on my back and decided to open and read Zoe and Em's message.

Hey Cay, Zoeeee speaking ☺, Em's still without internet which is driving her (and me) nuts, only joking. Love yur stuff, we wish we could be there too, bet it's tons more fun than here at the mo. Me and Em went out last night and 'cause the weather's been rubbishy (still is) hardly anyone was out. Sooooo boring. ☹ Nothing much to report really, need your news to cheer us up. Luv Zoeeee & Em xx

I definitely wasn't the right person to cheer them up, as much as I'd love to, but at least I could send them a pic of those guys putting up the stands.

Hi there, great to find your message ☺. Sending you a feel good pic of some guys without shirts, clearly gorgeous, don't you think? Took this especially for you back home so hope it brings you a bit of sunshine. Sorry this is going to be a tad short.... am on a bit of a downer too ☹. You'll see from the next pic I'm sending....and I think I've got flu coming just to make things worse ☹. Starting to regret everything. Cay xx

Through my window I could hear loads of noise, maybe it was people cheering somewhere in the distance, but anyway it was difficult to make it out with all the loud bangs and trumpets or something. I wanted to go and see what was happening but I wasn't sure if I could manage it or not. Wait a minute, didn't Joe say something about a horse trial? And if I can remember correctly, he basically suggested meeting near the florist at six o'clock, so I've still got plenty of time. I could have done with some cheering up.

Perhaps if I took some more tablets they'd put me back on track and even though I didn't understand the blurb on the packet of Tachipirina, I reckoned it was OK to take another couple of tablets by that time. Trouble was, I'd never bothered to read medicine instructions 'cause Mum was always there to check it out for me.

To think, it would've been so easy to call her and get all the sympathy and care I know she'd give me, but I hadn't dare call her; I'd totally ruin Mum and Dad's holiday.

Anyhow, I took the pain killers and eventually got myself changed, finally pulling my room door closed behind me at the same time as my phone just warned me that a new message had arrived I'd decided to open later. It was all very quiet in the, I wanted to say, bed and breakfast, but as there wasn't breakfast available, I had to say accommodation. No radio playing, no washing machine stuck on spin and no sign of the owner to check who was opening or closing his doors.

When I stepped down into the street, the August heat hit me, it was really quite overpowering and the sun made my sore and warty tattoo smart. A group of kids all wearing the same club scarves, overtook me running excitedly together along the street. I could see them up ahead overtaking or dodging other people walking in the same direction.

It was a massive effort for me to walk up and down the steep little streets and avoiding those who had stopped to window-shop along the way because the heat was really slowing me up. I was absolutely pooped. And what made it worse, was that I was trying to keep my wrist out of the burning sun.

I was feeling confused; didn't I read that the horse race was on the sixteenth? It wasn't the sixteenth already was it? I tried to work out the date today which I couldn't do, so I resorted to pulling out my phone to have a look. No it was definitely the thirteenth. As I got closer to the Piazza del Campo, there were so many people and so many voices intermingling with each other, it had become a mesmerising hum, for which I found myself being swept along.

'Caylin!' That had to be Joe shouting to me. I turned myself to look in the direction from which his voice came but there were too many people for me to pick him out and from where I was standing, I couldn't even see where the Florist shop was. Then I spotted his blond hair and his arm stuck up in the air waving at me.

'Caylin, wait there!' He shouted again. I nodded trying to move to one side so he could catch me up.

'My god, you feel OK?' he said staring at me, 'you look terrible.'

'Thanks mate,' I said forcing a smile, 'it's flu or something, anyway, I'll get over it. What's going on here?'

'I found out it's the beginning of the build-up to the horse race, apparently for three days they do trial races, then it's the biggy on the sixteenth.'

'Cool,' I said trying to sound enthusiastic, which was totally difficult for how I was feeling. I took some mouthfuls of water from my bottle.

'Someone told me that you can stand behind the barriers inside the centre of the square, and watch the race for free,' he said, 'otherwise, if you sit in the seats around the outside of the track, it'll cost a fortune. Have you seen photo's of the race?'

'Er, can't say I have,' I replied naively.

'Well, believe me, you're crammed in, and so they say with thousands of other spectators,' he said, 'I've seen the photo's so, yup you're crammed in all right.'

'Oh.' I said with the height of intelligence.

'I'm going to go into the centre, coming?' he corrected himself, 'I mean, if you feel up to it?'

'Um, of course,' I said. How could I be in Siena and not see anything that went on here. People pushed past us, I guessed they were eager to enter.

'Even though it doesn't start for an hour or so, apparently it's recommended to get a standing place well in time before they close the entrances,' he added.

People were still pushing past us which was becoming more and more annoying; well, to me anyway. It was time to move away from where we'd met.

'Come on, let's go.'

So he led the way through the crowds and into the centre of the Piazza del Campo. I could see from the tall tower behind me on the other side, that the time was five fifty in the afternoon and the sun was half in, half out of the square which thankfully would make standing more bearable in the shade, except that most people who like us, were heading towards the same shaded areas.

'Joe,' I managed to get out at the same time as tugging his T-shirt, 'I don't think I can stay here, I really don't feel that great.'

'I'm so sorry,' he replied, 'I shouldn't have dragged you here, come on, let's get you away.' He put his arm around my shoulders and guided me back through the people. If I wasn't feeling so nauseous, I think I probably would've enjoyed being taken care of by a tall, strong guy. But at that moment, all I could think about was leaving the square with all its noise and chaos and sitting down somewhere. The problem was, there were no seats.

That was it, I absolutely couldn't take another step and as gross as I would've normally found it, I slid down inside of a telephone shop entrance and sat on the dusty tiles with my back against a window. The shop door was open and inside I could see the look on the face of a guy as he was assisting a woman client. Thought he had a bit of a surprised expression.

'Here, drink your water,' Joe said, 'don't worry about the assistant, I'll speak to him if necessary. How are you feeling?'

'Horrible.' I was really sweating, I didn't think it was from the heat and my head pained me so much. I brought both my knees up to my chest and put my arms around them, burying my face into my long skirt.

I felt Joe take my right hand which made me lift my head up to see what he was doing; he wasn't holding my hand just in a caring kind of way, I realised he was peering at my wrist's disgusting warty tattoo.

'Caylin, you can tell me to mind my own, but I'd say you really need to get this looked at,' he said, 'and now.' He was looking at me so seriously that he was actually worrying me.

I glanced down at my wrist and well, yes I had to agree that it had become pretty bad. I didn't remember seeing the redness going up my arm like that before, or the scary looking bubbles. Sora had gone.

'Stay there,' Joe whispered. Ha, he needn't have worried, I wasn't going anywhere, in fact I didn't think I could've.

As I watched the people rushing past the shop entrance, nearly all of them followed their eyes down to me sitting on the floor before quickly hurrying along again. I must've looked like someone of no fixed address, or a dope-head even. What had I done to myself? I wanted to cry.

Joe waited his turn until he could speak to the guy behind the counter. I couldn't hear what was being said, but they both turned and looked at me with concern. *Oh please, come on, I'm not dying you know*, I thought.

Joe came back out of the shop and sat down next to me. He put his arm around me.

'He's calling the ambulance service,' he said. *Now you're frightening me*, I thought.

'There's loads of medics around because of the horse race trials and at least they can take a quick look at you.'

'I'll be fine in a few minutes,' I responded sitting myself up higher against the window, 'there's no need to call anyone, I can get something from the pharmacy.' But I knew that in reality, it was wishful thinking and I was trying to kid myself that nothing was really the matter.

There they were, two of them. *Thanks a bunch, Joe*, I thought. A man carrying a big holdall and a young girl appeared in the doorway, both of them looking down at me. They were wearing the bright yellowy-green trousers and tops, the outfits which really stood out brightly.

'Don't go, Joe,' I found myself saying quickly to him as he got up and stepped back to let them get nearer to me. He shook his head.

They put on some latex gloves and crouched down next to me.

'What you name?' The girl asked me and I told her.

'Have you had medicine today?' I had to think. I told her I took a couple of Tachipirina, even though I was certain I pronounced it in a strange way, at three thirty or four that afternoon. All the while she was asking me questions and making notes, the man was checking me when he also noticed my wrist. More questions.

It was explained to me that I needed to go to hospital to be checked more thoroughly and more than likely have a good dose of antibiotics. Great.

Next thing, the man had returned with a seat thing and I was lifted onto it and strapped in tightly. There really wasn't any need for that, surely.

Off we went, passing the crowds of people gathering to watch the horse race trial and there I was being wheeled away with Joe by my side and the ambulance looming in the distance. I turned towards Joe.

'Please don't tell *anyone*.' I exaggerated the *anyone* and I could tell he knew exactly who I meant when he put his hand on my shoulder and gave it a reassuring squeeze.

12

Guardian angel

Well that was totally unexpected. I'd just spent a night and nearly all today in the big hospital, Le Scotte; first in the Pronto Soccorso where I was prodded and poked, then in another ward in another part of that massive hospital complex.

It turned out that I had an acute reaction to the tattooing, more than likely the doctors said, to the coloured ink but they said it could also have been because the tattooist wasn't hygienic enough. They asked me where I had it done, but I actually couldn't remember where or which part of the old town. They even showed me a map, but it was impossible for me to recall where I went. Siena was a maze to me. Joe must've thought I was a really dumb person.

Anyhow, I'd been given loads of antibiotics and other stuff which will help my body fight against the disgusting warty and bubbly infection.

Joe stayed near me for most of the time (I spied him asleep once or twice), he must've been so bored, but he wasn't allowed to stay overnight. Said he found some seats in another waiting area where he tried to sleep until this morning. Eventually I was allowed to leave.

'I owe you for the shuttle bus to get back here from the hospital late this afternoon,' I said, 'I know, let me buy you a pizza this evening, in appreciation for all the help you've given me.'

'Sure you're up to it?' he asked, 'don't you think you should rest?'

'Nah, I feel a bit better and if I can get some shut-eye now for an hour or so, I should be in top form,' I replied grinning.

'We don't have a lot of time left on this holiday so I definitely don't want to waste any more of it,' I added. And what I did next not only surprised him but also myself.

'Mind facing the other way a sec,' I said.

'Um, no...'

I waited for him to turn round then I took off my long skirt and top leaving me in just my pants and bra. I flung my things over the bedroom chair, and feeling all giggly, I slipped under the bedclothes.

'OK, now you mustn't go getting the wrong idea, but you can turn around now,' I said, 'and if you're as tired as I am, you're welcome here next to me.' Was it really me saying that? I tried not to smile too much because he was having some sort of difficulty undoing his trousers; think he was rushing. Cor didn't he look sexy just in his tight black boxers and his whale tail pendant.

'How could I refuse a request like that,' he beamed, 'on my way.'

And so he got in beside me in the little single bed and turning on his right side to face my back he put his arm around me. I gently reached for my phone and set the alarm to go off in a couple of hours and nestled backwards into his warm body letting my bandaged wrist hang out over the side. Oh how comforting and reassuring it was to have him there with me, just like my guardian angel.

The alarm sounded at the time I'd set for seven this evening and switched it off before turning my body to face Joe. He gave me a warm smile. I cuddled into him and rested my bandaged wrist across the top of the bedclothes which were covering his chest and we laid listening to the sounds of drums and trumpets in the distance.

'How do you feel now? He asked me.

'Well enough for pizza.'

'That's good to hear, come on then let's go out and hit Siena.'

I was really happy that he wasn't making me feel embarrassed by watching me get dressed. Instead, he looked out of the little window allowing me time to sort myself out. I'd been worrying of how this was going to turn out, I mean, by getting into the same bed together and if he was going to expect me to have sex with him. And even though when we were lying there together, I had sensed his want, shall we say, but he hadn't pressurised me, not like those others I'd met. He was a true gentleman.

Joe returned to our table with our drinks and sat back down.

'Joe,' I said, 'what do your parents think about you coming to Siena to check me out?'

'They're not my parents,' he said just before taking a big bite of his pizza. I wasn't expecting him to come out with that.

'Oh, I'm sorry.'

'Sorry for what?' he half grinned.

'Er, sorry you're not with your true parents,' I was stuttering over my words.

'Don't worry, it's OK,' he replied, 'they're my adopted parents.'

'Oh, I see, but you're tall just like they are, you look like you're from the same family.'

'In reality that's right,' he said, 'Mum is in fact my auntie, she's my real Mum's older sister.'

I didn't know what to assume, and I was wondering if his parents were dead then, killed somehow. I probably had a lost expression as I wasn't sure what to say next when luckily Joe rescued me from a verbal disaster.

'Don't worry, it's a long story,' he said, 'maybe one day I'll bore you about my family and what my parents are doing in Australia.'

'Oh, wow Australia.'

So they were alive and kicking, but as I was wondering if it was a bit of a sore subject for him, I tried to search for something else to speak about. We continued eating for a couple of minutes when I piped up with another question.

'Mind if I ask how old you are,' I said, 'I mean, I like to guess peoples ages.'

He finished eating his mouthful of tuna pizza before he could answer.

'Sure, but whether I'll divulge the information is dependable,' he replied with a grin, and he went back to cutting another triangle of his pizza.

'Right then, I'd say you're around twenty, twenty-one, am I close?' Think I was feeling a bit better and cheeky.

'Clever,' he said, 'twenty-two next May.'

'Hum, let me see,' I said, 'that means you're either Taurus or Gemini.'

'Ah, so you're into horoscopes and all that then, I'm a bull,' he said with a laugh.

'And I'm a crab, I replied, 'pleased to have met you.' *In fact, very pleased to have met you.* Now that could be quite interesting. Joe caught me staring into space.

'Go on then, what can you tell me?' He had a twinkle in his eye.

'I think bulls and crabs are supposed to get along OK together.'

Did he really do that? I mean did he really raise his eyes in a way to imply that star signs were just a load of hooey? I'd love to look inside his head to know what he was thinking, actually better still, what he thought about me, you know, the girl who ran away from her parents on holiday, got branded a thief, cut and dyed her hair then got a tattoo which went all wrong and ended up in hospital. I'd been quite a dummy. And to add to that, I've made him imagine that I was weak enough to be controlled by star signs.

'OK, I admit to knowing the star signs, just the dates and stuff like that,' I said, 'but I don't read the horoscopes. Anyway, I wouldn't want to know whether tomorrow or next week, next year even, that something horrible could happen to me.'

'You mean it's better to take each day as it comes,' he said.

I wished I knew if he was referring to life in general or the time I was currently spending with him. Hum tricky.

'Yup,' I replied confidently. And he didn't know in what way I was referring to either.

Every now and again the music coming from the pizzeria's radio was over-powered by distant cheering from the second day of the horse race trials. Joe held up his glass of beer.

'Here's to Siena.'

'Yeah, here's and cheers to Siena,' I added as we clinked our glasses together. We then both continued to eat our pizzas, where occasionally I'd glance at him when he was looking down, to catch a glimpse of his short wisps of blond hair moving ever to slightly with the rhythm of the wobbling fan above our heads.

'*Grazie mille* for the pizza and beer,' Joe said whilst we strolled along the street.

'*Prego*,' I said. I'd been waiting to have the opportunity to be able to say *you're welcome* to someone since I'd found the translation in my dictionary. I think we'd both thought it funny since I didn't have a clue about the language or pronunciation.

Joe was walking with his right hand in his trouser pocket, so I took the chance that he wouldn't mind if I slipped my left arm through his. Nothing was needed to be said when he squeezed our arms together in confirmation that it was fine to do just that.

Maybe he knew I was tired and hanging a bit from the infection I was fighting, but one thing was certain, I was happy and I felt happy with everything. I loved the shop windows all lit up in the evening with the beautiful and sometimes expensive things inside. And again tonight, Siena was full of aromas, the leather, the perfumes, coffee and the restaurants.

'Quick, hide!' I grabbed Joe's arm and pulled him into a side street. I was sure that Lula was up ahead of us.

'What's the matter, who've you seen?'

'Lula who tells people I'm a thief, remember?'

Joe moved to the end of the building and carefully peered round the street corner, I peeped round from behind him. It was her all right.

'Shall we follow her?' I whispered.

'Why do you want to do that?'

'Just curious to know what she does I suppose.'

'Don't they say that curiosity killed the cat?'

'I'm a crab.'

'Funny.'

So keeping a safe distance we followed Lula, and every now and then we were having to hide ourselves among the tourists if she happened to stop. In fact, one time we had to wait for ages whilst she stopped to speak to someone on her phone. Then there was another time she was speaking to someone on her phone, I noticed that she was really agitated. Her voice was raised and at the same time she was moving her hands in a furious manner whilst she strode along. She seemed so intent that I didn't think she'd have noticed me if I'd stood there right in front of her. The phone conversation finished and we continued a bit further.

'Did you see that?' I said, 'did you see she almost knocked that man off his bike?'

'Yup, I don't think she bothered looking.'

'She's crazy.'

'Do you want to continue?' Joe asked me.

'I think it'll be OK as long as there's other people around and she doesn't see us. What say you?'

'Fair shout.'

Lula was hollering at someone on the phone again and when she'd finished she put her phone inside the back pocket of her jeans. Then she strutted along at a rate making it quite difficult for us to keep up.

I think we'd gone quite a way when we'd reached a two-way road on the outside of the old town and opposite a public garden area. Her phone rang and she took it out once again where it seemed like she was listening to someone on the other end. Well, she definitely couldn't have been concentrating on what she was doing; both Joe and me gasped as we watched her step out into the road and crossed to the other side. Luckily for her, the driver saw her just in time and swerved to miss her. You just can't j-walk in Italy.

Lula slowed her pace down and then she stopped near one of the stone benches. It seemed like she was looking for someone. Joe immediately pulled me to the side near some rose bushes making me feel giggly like I was an excited child trying to hide from a teacher to skive a lesson.

We could see an older couple walking along the pavement bedside the road; they'd walked past her, so it wasn't them she was waiting for. Then we saw a guy wearing jeans and T-shirt under a dark leather jacket approaching her. She noticed him and looking straight at him, waited until they were face to face.

With the help of the street light he looked unshaven and quite anxious. Who *was* he? I wondered.

'Oh my god, look at that.'

'Shush, she'll hear you,' Joe said.

I couldn't believe what I was watching; the guy was holding out his hand and Lula was handing a massive bundle of what looked like euro notes to him. They were speaking and I know that Joe was straining to listen which wasn't easy because just a short distance away was a large fountain gushing out water noisily into a big round basin. Lula and the guy hugged then parted.

We watched in silence as Lula walked away in the direction we'd followed her from, and the guy went across the road and entered into what looked like an alleyway.

13

Regrets

After we'd walked quite a way following Lula, I was really dead on my feet. It'd been such a long and tiring day and even my ankle was starting to get on my nerves; Joe was pretty much bushed too.

'Let's get a taxi,' Joe said and just as I was about to answer him,

'Cor, look at that,' he was pointing to the sky, 'a shooting star.'

'Great, I missed it,' I said disappointedly, 'aren't you supposed to make a wish?'

'Think you're right,' he said.

'Done.'

'You know, I'd really like to see one too, Mum said she saw some recently.

We both stared at the dark and clear night sky and I'd say within just five minutes, we'd seen three or four zoom past overhead. I made my wish.

'My place or yours, gorgeous?' Joe asked me. Well I didn't feel particularly gorgeous but the question was kind of funny. Anyway, that was a point, I thought, I hadn't known where *his place* was exactly.

'Do you mind if we stay at my place?' I asked, 'it's just that I've got my antibiotics and other stuff there too.'

'Course not,' he said, 'what's the street name again?'

'Er...' I was totally useless for the umpteenth time.

'It's OK, we can use google maps to find it.'
'Good idea,' I said.

After we'd let ourselves into my room and when Joe was looking at his phone, I found my toothbrush and went to the bathroom. I had to admit I was feeling nervous as at the back of my mind I was wondering if Joe was hoping we'd have sex. After all, this would be the second time he'd been in my bed; the first time being was when we got back from the hospital late in the afternoon when I needed to sleep before we went out.

When I returned to my room, Joe went to the bathroom and during that short time, I'd slipped quickly into the little bed. This time though, without any underwear. But I have to say, that was only because I didn't want to appear prudish and risk putting Joe completely off me.

Joe's face had a look of happy surprise when he came back as he saw my bra and pants that I'd taken off and left in an untidy heap during my rush. After he'd turned the light out, I watched him undress and I could tell from his silhouette that he'd taken everything off before slipping in next to me.

Almost immediately and without any hesitation, Joe began kissing me. We kissed for quite some time. It was like our lips were little magnets pulled together and not able to let go. It was incredible. And even though I felt comfortable with Joe, I still found it hard stopping myself feeling uneasy about having sex for the first time, and it wasn't just that; I hadn't known him for very long. I wasn't ready and how was I going to get round it? I could feel Joe's erection and I had to say something.

'Joe, um, I'm so sorry, I don't think I'm ready just yet.' I *was* sorry.

'Oh, don't worry, it's OK,' he said, 'only when you're sure.' He gave me a gentle kiss. I hoped he meant it and that I hadn't spoilt everything for him.

'I'm really happy you understand, Joe,' I said, 'thank you.' And feeling relieved and appreciative for his patience, I gave him a great big hug. He hugged me back without saying anything but sensing his disappointment; his quietness, I wondered if I was being really mean and uncaring. There I was all comfy in his arms and he knew he had to wait until I said *yes*. I was sure he had no idea I was a virgin.

I was spending my time with someone who'd come to find me, to see if I was OK, someone who looked after me when I wasn't feeling well and I'd just gone and probably made him feel unwanted. And he could've been really huffy with me and gone back to his place, but he didn't. He wasn't like those others.

'Joe?' I moved my mouth up towards his ear to whisper, 'would you like me to… you know... use my hand to…?'

'No, it's OK, Caylin, honestly, but thanks for the offer,' he said softly, 'I want to wait until you feel comfortable, I'm not going to rush you.'

He fell asleep before I did.

I don't think it would be mean to take a photo, would it? I thought to myself when I woke up. It wasn't to be mean or embarrassing, I just wanted to send it to the girls back home to show them just how nice he looked with his messed-up hair and the whale-tail pendant he still had fastened around his neck. Was it a gift from someone back home? I wondered. I couldn't help feeling a tinge of jealousy. I gently reached for my phone and took a sneaky pic of Joe asleep. The phone flashed when it took the photo but fortunately it didn't wake Joe up.

I wanted to try to go back to sleep for a bit longer but I couldn't so it was probably a good a time as any to catch up on my messages, I knew there were five waiting to be read.

Hello Caylin, Dad here, the young man Joe offered to go to Siena to check you were OK. Your mum was in a right state worrying about you and I couldn't convince her that you're independent enough to manage and that you're sensible (I hope) enough to know what's right and what's not. Naturally he contacted us to let us know he'd seen you. He seems a decent lad. If he hadn't had gone to look for you, I would've, but I guess you wouldn't have liked that. Looking forward to seeing you soon preferably before we're due to go to the airport! By the way, I've appreciated your concern over my problem with the cheese, which can be forgotten now thanks Caylin.

Cor, I didn't think I could imagine how things would have turned out if Dad had come to Siena to look for me. For a start, he would've had trouble recognising me and might have reported me as a missing person, then police would have been involved. Or, perhaps being an ex army Major he knew of clever ways in which to search out a person. What a thought. Then, when he'd discovered me, he would have probably frog-marched me back to the hotel and locked me up in anger because of what I'd done to myself.

Anyhow I still had to face Mum and Dad but at least I've got Joe who would vouch for what happened and why I went incognito. Yes that'd be good.

Hi Dad, thanks for your message. Yes Joe seems a good person. Anyway, enjoy the rest of your time in the hotel, it's chaotic here in Siena now with the big horse race happening tomorrow. Looking forward to seeing you too, Caylin xxx

Butterflies.

Hello Caylin, it's great to hear things are good for you there. You know I've been worried, but I'm more relaxed now I know that the young lad Joe has seen you. I'm not wishing my holiday away, but I'm looking forward to seeing you soon though. Don't worry about Dad and the cheese, he saw the funny side afterwards and all's forgiven. Oh yes, remember those two girls travelling together? Amazing luck for them yesterday...they bought a ten euro scratch card between them and immediately won a thousand euros! Somehow they managed to persuade the hotel manager to let them throw a pool party last night to celebrate. I can't swear on it, but I think they'd also invited a couple of Italian lads from somewhere! Those girls are so funny, wild but funny! It was a shame you weren't here, you would've liked it too. Speak again soon, Love Mum xxx

It was a good job they didn't know that I was lying in bed with Joe at that very moment of writing to them, and who was still asleep; I knew that because every now and then he twitched, making me jump. I wondered what he was dreaming about. I'd better reply to Mum.

Hi Mum, thanks for your message, yes things are OK here and don't worry I'm looking forward to seeing you too ☺. I remember those girls, I bet they livened the place up a bit, loved to have been a fly on the wall. I've nothing particularly exciting to report back to you, except there's a lot of TV cameras here setting up for the big race tomorrow. Maybe you'll find it on your hotel TV and maybe you'll see me ☺ Lots of love, Caylin xxx

I didn't think so though, and moreover, I hoped they wouldn't. Right then, Zoe and Em. I opened Zoe's first, and she'd sent two.

What...is...that? Actually, you don't need to tell me, I know what it is, it's a tattoo gone horrendously wrong. I've seen photos like that on FB, Cay. What was it meant to be? Zoeeeee xx

Zoe seemed angry. I'd better open her other message, here goes.

Cay, I'm sorry I was/am shocked to see that photo ☹. How are you? Have you been to the doctors yet? You have to, you have to get something like antibiotics or something. I hope it hasn't got any worse. Don't want you to get ill. Let me know as soon as poss how you are, Zoeeeee xx. PS The pic you've sent of those guys is now my phone's lock screen!

I was dreading opening Em's.

Have you gone way off your trolley Cay? Tattoo, right? It looks terrible, but why did you do it? I've looked it up now I'm back on the internet again and I've read that you should always go to a place where it's popular and so busy that you have to make an appointment in which case, I don't think you would've had time as you're only there a while, so I'm guessing it wasn't like that ☹. Seems like you've got an infection. I'm sorry if I'm putting a huge downer on things, but what about your parents, your Dad, oh Cay I feel for you. I hope you've seen a doctor and you're feeling better. Thanks for the pic, nice guys ☺. Look after yourself better Cay, hope to hear from you soon, Em x

Just as I expected; that was our Em all right.

Hi Guys, first, I'm sorry I have to reply to you both together and not separately as you both deserve. You are both real good friends and I'm so glad I know you, I'm dead lucky that you care so much about me ☺. You know it's vice versa too. Second it's a long, long story (I'll fill you in properly when I'm back) but I'm getting better with drugs ☺, the antibiotic type ☹. Remember that guy on our trip I sent you a photo of way back? He's here in Siena with me ☺☺ and we saw that psycho girl last night handing over loads of dosh to a guy and probably it's the dosh she blamed me for stealing ☹. Anyway the plot's getting interesting, I want to find out more about her. Third, take a look at the next pic I took a few mins ago, don't worry, it's nothing like the one of my wrist. AND I have to tell you, that it's all completely innocent. He's been a terrific guardian angel ☺, took me to hospital and he hasn't even pressurised me for you know what. All in good time I say. Gotta go 'cause I need to take some drugs ☺. Love you both, Cay xx

An intense gushy feeling swept through me. How privileged I was to know such caring people, including the tall blond male lying there next to me. I checked the time on my phone, it was nine thirty-five. I decided to go and have a shower and get dressed before Joe woke up.

I carefully tipped myself out of the little bed, plucked the towel hanging from the hook on the back of the bedroom door then turned the key to let myself out into the hallway. The bathroom was free and this morning, someone had actually opened the window to air. I pulled the light cord to switch the light on and stopped to look at myself in the mirror. I knew that I'd been a fool, all done on the spur of the moment without a second thought.

I sat on the loo and stayed there for a while thinking. Back home, a lot of people had said how much they liked my natural long auburn hair. I hadn't liked it that much when I was young but over time it literary grew on me especially as I hadn't known many people with the same natural colour; it was a bit different. Mum had said that my grandma had auburn hair too.

And when I'd sometimes flicked through the magazines belonging to the hairdressers where I helped, I'd noticed there were loads of hair models also with long auburn hair and now it was too late; I'd gone and messed up. My hair was short, black and sticking up in every direction.

I'd seen girls and women go in and have a complete change of style and colour, all done for different reasons, and then the following week they were back again wanting to revert to their original colour. It wasn't a quick process either. Sometimes the stylist would put a lot of light foils in to break up the colour and add more foils the next time and the next, or she'd use the strong colour strippers which could be a bit hit and miss. And if the style had been too short, no way could the hairstylist do much to change anything there, so like me, they had to live with it.

Now I had the extra worry about my infected tattoo. I had no idea what it'll look like when or if it eventually healed. I loved Sora, but couldn't stand seeing that mess on my wrist. I couldn't help but cry, I'd been a right idiot.

I remembered I'd left Joe in the bedroom and wondered if he was still asleep. I had to pull myself together before he came looking for me. I didn't want him to see me like this so I wiped away the *sorry for myself tears* and blew my nose before running the shower with great anticipation on how I'd manage keeping my horrid tattoo dry.

I opened the bedroom door to see Joe standing in his boxers near the window which he'd already opened and was pushing the shutter outwards allowing the warm morning air to drift in.

'Good morning,' he greeted. His lovely smile immediately replaced my negative spirit with one of gladness. Glad that he was there.

'*Bon jorno*,' I replied trying to appear bright and cheerful.

'How are you feeling?'

'Tons better,' I said, 'those drugs are fantastic.' I pointed to my packet of antibiotics.

I wasn't properly dry and I was just about managing to hold my towel around me whilst closing the door with my foot. One slip and I'd be mortified at showing all of myself to him as I had no secret plan to accidently on purpose drop my towel; yet.

When Joe returned from having a shower I was already dressed. I'd been thinking about Lula and that guy last night, and since we'd seen him go into an alleyway, I was eager to suggest about going back there. Only to see, I told him.

'I don't suppose it'll hurt if we take a look,' he said.

'Wonder where it leads?' he asked. We were both standing at the entrance to the gap in between the two buildings.

'One way to find out,' I replied throwing him a *oh please, can we?* look.

The only way to have described it was that it was a disgusting narrow alleyway with a steep descent stinking of pee and pigeon poo. We had to be extremely careful not to slip on the damp and green mossy covered paving as we descended between the tall stone buildings either side. It was obvious that the sun hardly touched this alleyway and surely it was utterly pointless in hanging out clean washing on the lines above. It was pigeon paradise.

It became apparent from the cigarette ends and rubbish discarded that people used it as a cut-through to reach a street in view at the bottom. That street was also jam-packed with tall narrow buildings but at least the sun reached it. We strolled along the one-way street for a while.

'Oh, come on Joe, this is pointless,' I said, 'let's go back.'

'I didn't like to say anything.' I ignored his comment.

So we turned and started strolling in the opposite direction when up ahead we could see someone stepping out through a doorway onto the street.

The guy who was then facing into the entrance was speaking to someone. A woman's voice could be heard and then a child's.

'Hey, do you reckon that's the guy?' Joe asked.

'Could be,' I said clutching at straws, but I didn't really have a clue.

'Umm, and from here, maybe *there is* a bit of a resemblance of who we saw in the gardens last night,' said Joe, 'come on, let's be tourists and go up past them.'

I took out my phone like we were looking at google maps and Joe was pointing in different directions as if we were searching for somewhere. I looped my arm with Joe's and as we got a bit closer, their tense voices could be heard quite distinctly. Every now and then, a little girl interrupted them whilst she played with a dolls pram she'd dragged outside until, who I assumed was her mother, said something and the little girl immediately sat on the step in silence.

The couple were so engrossed with their discussion long after we'd gone by, I actually didn't think they'd even realised that we or anyone else had walked past.

When we reached the top of the street, we turned and watched the guy bend down and kiss the little girl on the head, hug the woman and left via the stinky alleyway.

'You'll never guess,' Joe said with a look like he was trying to tease me.

'Oh go on then,' I said, 'what juicy gossip have you discovered?

'They're not Italian.'

'*Really?*' I said, 'that's not quite what I expected you to say.'

'And which now makes sense to me,' he said, 'why I couldn't get what him and Lula were saying to each other last night in the gardens.'

'But what language is it? Where are they from?'

'I honestly don't know.'

'So; Lula, that guy, woman and little girl are all connected somehow,' I said, 'and that could mean then, that when I stayed the first night with Lula, Vico her boyfriend and another guy, it couldn't have just been Italian I was hearing. I'd never had known, it all sounds the same to me.'

14

What a whopper

We were back in the room again and I was sitting on the bed with my legs crossed in a world of my own sketching Sora with her new short and dark spiky hair. This time I'd sketched her with tears in her beautiful eyes because she was also regretting having her long auburn hair cut. It took me a while before I realised that Joe had said something to me.

'I'm sorry, what?'

'Do you want to go and see the last horse race trial this evening?' asked Joe, 'or would you prefer to go to the main event tomorrow?'

'Or both?' I replied.

'If you're up to it, sure.'

'Nah, only kidding,' I said, 'I think I can wait now until the biggie tomorrow, I feel good though.'

As I was speaking, even then there were sounds of drum beats and chanting voices somewhere in the distance.

'Tell you what, I wouldn't mind a plate of pasta this evening, I think I've eaten quite enough pizza for a while.'

'Yeah me too,' he said patting his firm abs.

'Listen, it's not even twelve o'clock,' he said, 'fancy hiring a bike for a couple of hours?'

I was just about to reply.

'You *can* ride a bike can't you?' *The cheeky devil*, I thought. I playfully thumped him, leaving him with a dead arm and jumped off the bed in case I got one back. He moaned with the pain and rubbed it frantically, but I knew he was just fooling around. We put some footwear on again and went out.

'I'll ask for some information in that shop over there,' he said, 'see if they know where we can hire a couple of bikes, come on.'

We went over to a newsagents and Joe went on inside whilst I stayed outside to look at the racks of Siena souvenirs on display. I'd better think about what I could buy for Zoe and Em, also I was sure Mum would have liked something from there too. Well, there didn't seem to be a short supply of all the usual stuff like T-shirts, mugs, peaked caps, fridge magnets as well as amazing pictures of the horse race, I guessed was last years. I'd think about what I could get them, I still had time. Joe came back outside.

'Apparently Siena has a bike-sharing scheme, called something like SiPedala and the woman told me that there's a place where we can go to organise the hire,' he said, 'but they could be closed today because it's a bank holiday here.'

'Oh, a bank holiday?' I said, 'you'd never think it with all these shops open.'

'But she also said that there's an app which I can download onto my phone instead, if they're shut.'

'Sounds good to me.'

Miraculously we found a place to park our bums and went through the process of downloading the app successfully. Then Joe managed to locate the places in Siena where we could find the bikes and also how to pay online. I was glad he knew what he was doing. I'd had probably given up.

'Well, there's actually a place near the Fortress it says here, which incidentally is close to where we were watching Lula and the guy last night.'

I hadn't noticed the Fortress but that was probably because it was dark and I was more intent on seeing what she was up to handing over that money.

'It also tells us that there are three bikes left available at that place,' he said, 'shall we go for it?'

'What ya waiting for.'

When we reached the bike collection point, there were only two left, the ones Joe had luckily reserved online. The bikes were very modern-looking and I liked the grey baskets on the back.

'Where are the gears, Joe?' I asked whilst standing astride my large white bike, 'and what does this do?

'Hang on a minute,' he said whilst reading some instructions, 'OK, I understand now.'

Joe explained a couple of things to me, and one which really appealed to me was the fact that somehow the bike electronically helped you go up hills. All you had to do was press a button when the power was needed. Bit different to the one I had a few years ago.

'Cool,' I said.

Although it was a national bank holiday in Italy, nobody seemed to stay at home, and it struck me just how many car drivers were trying to find a place to park. There was no chance in this part, it was jam-packed.

Before we set off on our bikes, we pushed them over to an area near a kiosk and a bar where groups of people were looking at the view. From there, on the other side of a small valley you could see the massive black and white marble cathedral with its tower and to the left there was a huge brown coloured church. It was a good enough place as any to take a selfie with Joe; I got out my phone and hoped he wouldn't mind.

I took a shot of the view then I turned to put my back to the cathedral across the way and sidled closer to him at the same time as he turned to see where I'd gone. I moved my arm to get the phone in a good position in front of us.

'Come on,' I said.

'If you must,' he sighed. I sensed he forced a smile.

'Sure it's OK?'

'Yes, go on.'

So I took the shot.

'Look, it's come out nice,' I said, 'Mum and Dad would like to see that one...' and just as I was saying that, I had a terrible feeling creep over me fixating me to the spot.

'but?' he said.

'but, they can't, not yet, they haven't seen my hair,' I said. 'What am I gonna do?'

We were still leaning against the wall and he put his arm around my shoulder.

'We'll get round it somehow, now let me see this photo.'

I handed him my phone so he could see it properly but by then, the phone's display had returned to a different screen. He swiped the screen to get to the menu and touched the gallery symbol. *Oh no*, I thought.

It wasn't difficult to see the recent pictures I'd taken, and from where I was standing I could spy the one I'd taken of the guys putting up the barriers, and the one of him I'd taken on our first day when the coach had stopped at that little town. I moved only my eyes to look at Joe and to check his expression. I could've died.

'That's not on, Caylin.' Joe used a serious and disappointed tone.

He was looking at the shot I'd taken of him only that morning when he was asleep next to me.'

'I'm sorry...'

'Please don't do that.'

My heart felt very heavy with the fear I'd gone and blown it. A few moments ago I was worrying about what Mum and Dad would say about my hair, and now, I was in a turmoil over upsetting Joe. I had to remedy the situation. He was about to delete the photos of himself. *Why?* I wondered. I snatched my phone out of his hand, to stop him.

'And please don't *you* do that,' I said angrily, 'I like how you look, I like your blond hair especially in the morning and I like your pendant.'

He could take that how he wanted.

'And I like being with you.'

There, I'd said it.

Two or three older-looking tourists weren't standing that far away from us, and I caught one of the women's eyes and going by her sympathetic expression, I guessed they'd heard everything; how embarrassing. That put me in a bit of a strop.

'We'd better go,' I said as I haughtily yanked my bike off the path and onto the road followed by Joe. He caught hold of my handlebars stopping me from going any further.

'Look, it doesn't matter,' he said, ' I just don't like photos of myself that's all.'

'Well, you've nothing to worry about, you look perfectly fine to me,' I replied.

'You know,' I said, 'girls love to be with tall guys if that's what bothers you.'

I had to stop speaking and digging myself deeper into a hole at the expense of making him feel more uncomfortable; he might not have even been thinking about his height.

'Come on,' I said putting my bag into the basket, 'which way shall we go?'

'Hum, I think it'll be best if we try to avoid Piazza del Campo, bound to be chaotic again,' he said, 'let's go past those market stalls and stadium over there and then round to the left after that brown church and see where it takes us.'

It'd been ages since I'd ridden a bike, so I was quite wobbly and giggly.

'Don't forget to keep on the right,' he shouted from behind.

I'd forgotten about that; I was more intent on wondering how my bum looked.

We'd cycled past a place like a bus station on the right-hand side and on the left was a huge hotel and next to that were loads of market stalls in a park area. But we didn't stop, we went off the road to the right and slipped down a narrow street. From then, I spent most of my time laughing and ringing my bell, warning people I was coming.

We just kept on peddling around all the different streets without any particular aim, some even the wrong way and just enjoying the freedom and ease of getting around. I started to recognise where we were and I slowed down and then stopped. Joe pulled up alongside me.

'What's wrong?'

'I sort of recognise this street, I'm not sure if this is where I stayed with Lula and Vico,' I said, 'let me see.'

The club flags were of the design I recognised, orange and white with a unicorn. I let my bike roll along some more until I could see the parking area which was definitely where I remembered Vico had parked his car. Every parking space was filled but it was impossible for me to describe the type of car he had. I recalled that the apartment was in a building up the road from the parking area, so we had to be close to it.

'I think this is it.' I looked up to the opened first floor kitchen and bathroom windows and where my All Stars had been hidden. The downstairs wooden door was ajar slightly and leaning with my bike, I pushed it open some more. The smell of the unkempt apartment lingered inside the hallway.

'Look at this,' Joe whispered. He was pointing to the door buzzers fixed to the outside stone wall. There were two, one blank with no name, I guessed an empty apartment, and the other had two hand-printed surnames, one underneath the other.

'V. *Lorenzini*,' he read, 'definitely Italian.'

It sounded nice the way he pronounced *Lorenzini*, kind of swirly.

'That must be Vico then,' I said, 'and the other?'

'L. Hoxha, however you pronounce it, which I don't think is,' he said, 'because I'm sure that the Italians don't pronounce the letter H and I'm positive there's no Italian surnames beginning with H either.

'Oh.'

That had to be Lula then, whichever country she came from.

To our surprise we heard voices coming from inside the apartment; I didn't think anyone was at home it'd been so quiet. The voices, one I thought was that of Lula and the other belonging to Vico were increasing in volume and then they were shouting at each other and with what sounded like plenty of cupboard or door slamming going on.

'They're arguing in Italian,' Joe said.

We stayed at the bottom of the stairs with our bikes poised ready for a quick getaway if necessary. Joe was listening whilst pretending to check his bike tyres.

'I'll tell you what's being said when we're away from the area.'

'Is it bad?'

'Could be,' he said, 'watch out, someone's coming.'

It was too late, Vico hurtled down the stairs and swung the bottom door wide open revealing us directly outside. I was glued to the spot and unable to turn away in time. He glared at me and then to Joe and back to me again where he lingered a long time. He asked me a question but I couldn't respond in Italian except stutter in English. Joe said something in Italian, but I thought that his Bristolian accent was what must've finally gave him away and Vico put two and two together.

He went right up close to Joe who almost fell backwards over his bike. A lot of words were exchanged and I could sense that poor Joe was having trouble trawling up the words he needed in a hostile situation. He'd studied the language but I bet he hadn't thought he'd needed to study how to stand up for himself in Italian. My heart was pounding; I was terrified.

What came next made me cry. That monster Vico swung a punch with his right fist and caught Joe's left eye, sending him out into the street where he managed to stay upright but was bending over holding his face. I was absolutely stunned.

Vico glared at me then legged it down the road to the parking area and got into a car. And who should come down the stairs, but Lula. She'd been crying too. The three of us stood outside in the street and watched Vico rev the car's engine and pull away.

'It's all my fault,' I cried, 'I shouldn't have said anything about staying with them, and if I hadn't had accepted the lift with them in the first place, none of this would've happened. Actually, if I hadn't even come to Italy.'

'I'm OK,' he said, 'calm down Caylin, it's going to be OK.'

Both our bikes were lying on the ground and I was hugging Joe when I heard footsteps rushing down the stairs again making us look towards the door. To my surprise it was Lula with a bag of frozen peas, probably the same I'd used on my ankle. She held the bag out to Joe.

'*Grazie*, thanks,' he said and took the peas and held them against his left eye. She made a gesture for us to go up into the apartment, but we both shook our heads and thanked her again.

'Sorry,' she said. And she *did* look sorry.

I felt terribly confused and wanted to know what the arguing was about and what had been said between Vico and Joe, but I had to try to be patient; Joe was hurting.

We picked our bikes up off the ground and pushed them up the street in silence. Easy for me; Joe had to keep the peas on his eye with one hand which I thought was making him more agitated, if that was possible of course. For a split moment I thought Joe had gone all weird when he started laughing really loudly, quite scarily. He hadn't said much since he was landed one by Vico, but I knew he was dead angry. I wanted to say something but I was worrying about his reaction.

'Joe, I want to stop a moment,' I said, 'can we talk please.'

He didn't reply but he stopped still.

'What were they arguing about?'

Joe manoeuvred the wet bag of peas into a different position and changed hands. I patiently waited.

'I could hear that her spoken Italian wasn't as fluent as his,' he said, 'then I sort of understood that she has a brother somewhere who I gather Vico doesn't like much, called him a scrounger or something like that and of course she was defending him.'

'But what was he saying to you when he found us outside his door?'

'He said he's had money go missing from his apartment around the time you stayed and apparently it's still happening, and now that he's recognised you, and we were outside his apartment, you can imagine what he's assuming. He's raging *and* confused as I'd found out.'

'Well that makes most of us then,' I said.

Joe kicked a wall in frustration.

'Do you know how it feels when you can't state your case quick enough in another language?'

I didn't, but I could certainly imagine.

I put my bike against the wall and went over to cuddle him tightly. I thought that'd be better than my pathetic words. He felt really tense.

'And so what do you think of me now, you know, shouldn't Taurus the bull be tough?' He kissed my head.

'You're a good person Joe,' I said, 'and even though that Vico deserves a great big thump, he'll more than likely get it sooner or later. Anyway, he didn't exactly stand there waiting for you to smack him one, if you remember, he hot-footed it quick to his car, remember? He obviously wasn't going to wait to find out what your bull capabilities were.'

Joe relaxed his muscles.

'I'm really proud of you for not chasing him down the road like a raging bull,' I said, 'he's the one who look's a right what's it.'

I hated seeing fights and whenever there was something brewing between guys at a pub, even at the bowling centre, when they started pushing each other around I'd drag whoever I was with away to another area. I remember Dad telling me that he'd seen some terrible fights between the soldiers. I just hated that sort of thing.

'Now let me see that eye of yours.' I said.

'Wow!'

15

One Mojito too many

After the disaster yesterday, neither of us felt like going out and eating pasta; I was still tired from the infection and Joe's eye had finally closed over with the swelling. In the end we had to discard the soggy bag of defrosted peas. We'd taken our bikes back and picked up some bread with fillings and collected some stuff from my room. Oh, and we bought an icepack from a pharmacy and a piece of white gauze.

So there I was lying in *his* bed this time, and without any pressure to have sex, and waking up to the sun this morning which never seemed to fail, sending little golden lines through the shutter's slits onto the white walls. Joe was sleeping so I reached for my phone to check my messages where I could see there were two waiting.

Cor Cay, that's my girl ☺ but what's wrong with the guy? You're gonna have to take the lead sooner or later b4 your time runs out, Zoeeeee xx How's the tattoo?

Hum, I wasn't sure about that.

Hi Cay, seems you found yourself a good catch if you ask me, cor, can't be many guys around who'll cuddle up with you without expecting something in payment, Em x PS. Hope you're feeling better and that mess on your wrist is improving.

I thought I'd time to send quick replies.

Dear Zoe, the tattoo's still gruesome ☹ but luckily I'm starting to feel better thanks to the drugs ☺. Joe's not putting any pressure on and as I'm in no rush it's fine by me. Hey guess what? He's sporting a black eye which he didn't deserve ☹, all fun and games here. Got any gossip? Catch you soon, Cay xx

Dear Em, Yeah I think so too, even though he's got a black eye ☹, talk about him being in the wrong place at the wrong time! Feeling bit better thanks but the mess is still disgusting. Anyway, the sun's shining as usual so it's boring, I miss the Bristol clouds, ha only joking ☺ , any news for me? Cay xx

I put my phone down and turned onto my left side to look at Joe and his poor puffy and bruised eye. A thought occurred to me; I wondered if he had in actual fact, secretly wished it had been his nose that took the impact of that Vico's right fist. And if that'd been the case, maybe he'd hoped he'd get a nose job back in the UK under some kind of insurance scheme or something. He made me jump out of my skin.

'What are you staring at?' he asked, squinting at me through his one good eye, 'stupid question I guess.' There, he answered himself. He sounded very fed-up.

'Have you noticed on our bedroom walls and even in some shops, there's often a crucifix with Jesus?' I asked.

'Sure I have, you know they're very religious here,' he said, 'there's also a bible in the drawer over there.'

'Hum, it's not my thing though,' I said.

Ah yes, I remember one in the hotel of which I'd torn out a piece of paper to write a note to Mum and Dad.

'Even the Palio horse race has a religious connection where I believe every church in Siena has its own club. Even the horses go inside their club's church to receive a blessing before the race.'

'Strange,' I said, 'isn't it the proper race today?'

'Yup early this evening I think,' he said, 'and before then, I think there'll be a lot of parades too. We ought to go, it'll be our last opportunity seeing as we hadn't made any of the horse race trials.'

'Let's go for it.'

Joe's bed and breakfast, without the breakfast, was a few streets away from mine, and it was just the same outside with groups of youngsters running along wearing their silky coloured scarves. Siena never seemed to stop partying. Today though, the atmosphere felt much stronger than the previous three days; this time there were separate groups of women and men chanting and blowing whistles. It was quite exciting.

'We'll have to get to the Piazza del Campo early this afternoon so we can get into the centre part again,' he said, 'think you'll be OK this time?' I could tell that Joe was concerned rather than teasing me.

'Of course, I have my guardian angel with me.' That comment brought a smile to his face.

We hurried ourselves getting ready to go out, ending with the final touches, to Joe's eye. He held the white gauze square over his eye whilst I stuck it with some tape. At least it looked like he'd had something done to his eye in hospital instead of having been walloped. We stood together in front of a mirror.

'Cor, look at us,' he said.

'Speak for yourself,' I replied, thumping his arm.

We looked a sorry sight, but didn't we laugh.

It seemed like the whole world had descended onto those narrow streets and all heading in one direction, and for one thing only, the Palio. Children were perched on parent's shoulders which was probably the safest place for them at that time with all that pushing and shoving.

Quite often the local people wearing the silky coloured scarves didn't worry if they'd bumped into us or made us separate. I was lucky though, because it was easy to spot Joe partly for his height but mainly today it was the white gauze over his eye which vividly stood out.

We were subjected to more pushing and shoving until we were obliged to step quickly into a boutique doorway sensing something was coming by. It was an immense group of people following a man on foot who was struggling to keep a tall and lean horse under control through the crowds. The men, women and children were running in front, at the side and behind that poor horse which was tugging its head against the reign; its eyes very scared and wild.

I imagined that the same thing was happening along all the streets leading from each club to the Piazza del Campo and each horse drenched in sweat and fear.

We continued to walk along again until we came across a small supermarket where in its window, was a giant piece of juicy roast pork being sliced and put into pieces of bread.

'Got to get some of that,' Joe said.

'I'll second that.'

The lady behind the delicatessen counter smiled at me and chatted sympathetically with Joe whilst she sliced the thick pieces and laying them onto the bread. I wondered if she felt sorry for him having had a gauze over his eye and I hoped too, that she'd give us extra pork because the meat looked super scrummy with its coating of rosemary and salt seasoning.

We stepped back outside into the Palio mayhem clutching our rolls and cold bottles of peach flavoured iced tea. Then almost immediately, we were forced again to get into a shop doorway, this time a classy-looking shoe shop with its strong smell of leather, to wait for an approaching emergency vehicle to pass. Its strange Italian siren was deafening.

The ambulance driver was frantically beeping the horn at the people who were dawdling along in front of it as if nothing really mattered. I solemnly wondered where the ambulance could have been heading; was it a child or was it an old person who needed their life saved and I too wanted to shout at those dawdlers to get out of the way. It gave me the shivers; life or death.

Well, we survived the Palio, and that wasn't an understatement by the way. Finally after having dodged horses, annoying pushchairs, dawdlers and groups of chanters, we arrived at the Piazza del Campo where we could see the centre was already packed with spectators and we just about got in before the police closed the entrances, meaning nobody else could enter and nobody could get out until the race had finished. Joe found out from a person next to him that there weren't any loos, so you had to hold on or pee yourself. Perhaps it *was* pee I walked through on our way back to the exit. How gross.

I thought that the only other time I'd been to an event with that many people was when I saw David Guetta but that had a different atmosphere. There, everyone was chanting for him and his guests, but at the Palio it was full of serious rivalry between the clubs. I reckoned that some of the men, even women were asking for trouble with the way they were taunting others.

We'd struggled to squeeze past people to get as close to the barriers as we could but of course, most of the people wanted those places too. Anyway, even with loads of others in front of us, luckily we could still see bits of what was happening. It was an amazing event with medieval costume parades and flag waving and drum beating and trumpeters even though we hadn't had a clue of what the significance was for some of the rituals. But for me, the best bit was when the Carabinieri police on horses charged around the track at full pelt with their swords out, just like they were going into battle.

As for the race itself, it shocked me. The riders were violently pulling those poor horse's mouths with the bridle and they were kicking the horse's sides dead hard to make them go faster and if that wasn't enough, they whipped them with their sticks; sometimes they whipped each other. And I remember screaming when we saw a horse slam into a padded wall as it was being ridden round a bend at top speed and it fell down which was horrible to see. I didn't feel sorry for the rider who was lying on the dirt and then dragged over the barriers just in time before the other horses came round again and stamped on him. In all, I'd say that the Palio was a showcase of barbaric frenzy and beauty rolled into one.

'Fancy seeing if we can find a place to eat some pasta?' asked Joe.

'Yeah, I bet the atmosphere will be pretty incredible out tonight.'

We didn't bother going back to change, and I was relieved because if I'd laid down, I'd had probably fallen asleep and missed all the Palio celebrations, so that was fine by me.

It'd felt like we'd walked for miles in and around the little streets searching for an available table in a restaurant. Nearly every eating place we passed including Indian and Chinese had people queuing outside. We only needed a little table for the two of us which seemed near on impossible and just when we were on the point of giving up, we found one.

It was at a really cute and tiny trattoria with eight small wooden tables inside and ours was positioned quite close to the window.

'Come on,' I said, 'let's swap seats.'

'No, it's OK, no big deal.'

'I'd prefer it if we swapped Joe, then at least you can get on and enjoy your meal without the gawkers annoying you.'

I'd got used to seeing poor Joe with the white gauze over his eye, so I didn't really take a lot notice. We swapped places and this time I was facing out towards the street.

Every now and then, hundreds of celebrators walked past the window blowing whistles, singing and beating drums and basically making as much noise as they could. I supposed they must've been the winning club which had a black and white flag with a wolf in the middle and everyone of them were wearing matching silky scarves.

It was actually difficult to concentrate on a conversation or hear what the waiter was saying for all the noise and confusion outside. Loads of them were going past in the same colours holding up a massive banner. It seemed never ending and I bet it was fun being part of one of those clubs, especially if you won the Palio and probably terrible if you lost.

I devoured my plate of pici pasta with a bacon and tomato sauce before Joe finished his and from where I was sitting, I could spy a cabinet with cakes and desserts of which one in particular caught my eye; *the tiramisu*.

So, we then polished-off a couple of those and washed it all down with half a bottle of white wine and by that time I was feeling quite stuffed. The waiter, who was wearing a gorgeous aftershave, didn't check we wanted it, but he then brought out two small ice cold glasses with a yellow liquor called Lemoncello, which I'd decided just had to be my favourite liquor. Feeling very slightly under the influence and smiley, Joe, who'd had more wine than me, was also looking like a happy cat. But seeing as the happy cat wouldn't let me pay for my half, I left a decent tip for the waiter, who incidentally was quite nice.

'Thanks Joe,' I said, 'that was lush.' I sort of jumped onto my tip toes to give him a kiss on his cheek, but instead I misjudged it and hit my head on his bad eye. I knew it hurt because his good eye was watering. I could've died I felt so bad, and all he did was told me he was fine.

'What do you think about going to see where they're celebrating the win and probably getting wrecked?' Joe said.

'Not probably,' I replied looping my arm inside his as we started to stroll along again, 'yeah, could be a bit of fun to join in.'

'Hum, don't know about that,' he said, 'but could be fun trying.'

So, we caught up with a noisy group of celebrators and cheekily followed along behind them until we eventually ended up at one of their hangouts, and where there were those long wooden tables and bench seats of which almost all were being occupied. It was still evident that they'd eaten as not all the tables had been cleared of their dirty plates, but amongst all their cheering and singing, the women from the kitchen were gradually getting on top of it all.

It looked to me that most of the teenagers were riding high on emotion while some of them and the older ones were getting rowdy from all the wine and beer they were buying from inside their hangout and taking to their tables.

For ages, I'd been really wanting to try that Mojito cocktail I'd seen so many people sipping through straws and when I was at that bar with Stefania the other day, I watched the barman prepare it. I was sure he used white rum, mint, ice, sugar and fizzy water.

'Let's get something to drink,' I suggested to Joe.

'Why not,' he said, 'gotta get into the spirit of things.'

'Funny.'

We waited our turn amongst so many people, occasionally our feet getting trod on or we became separated moving out of the way for someone with a tray of drinks, until we eventually got served.

'Oh Joe,' I said, 'try this, it's heavenly.' It was difficult not to sip gigantic mouthfuls of the Mojito cocktail through the black straw.

'No I'm fine with beer, thanks.' He put his hand up as a gesture he didn't want to taste it, whilst he took a couple of long swigs from his glass.

We were fortunate that when we went outside again, that we were able to grab a couple of seats. Everyone there was so ecstatically happy that their club had won the Palio, I didn't think they cared that we'd joined them, but what was a shame though, was that we both didn't have one of their scarves to wave around and to feel really part of it.

Out of curiosity, I checked my phone to see what the time was; it was eleven thirty five and it was busier than ever with hardly any room for standing let alone sitting. I fancied another Mojito, so I sent Joe back inside whilst I sort of lounged across his seat so to guard it from being taken. I wasn't afraid to go and ask at the bar, but what I was afraid of was being asked for proof I was over eighteen.

I spied Joe and his white gauze picking his way through the people and trying not to spill our drinks. I stood up and waved.

'Over here!' I shouted. My eyes met with a couple of noisy girls around my age, maybe a little older. *Yup, we're English*, I thought. They both still had dark sunglasses perched on top their heads and they were wearing very short shorts with cut-off T-shirts revealing their brown tummies, and I couldn't help noticing one had a belly button piercing shining under the party lights. I wanted to see what they were wearing on their feet, but I guessed it would have been bumper boots, the same as most of the others.

Joe joined me at the table again.

'Can I take a picture of us please Joe,' I asked very nicely with a cheesy grin.

'I suppose so.'

I took out my phone and held it on the table in front of us. We moved in closer together and I pressed the button a couple of times. On the screen we saw those girls behind us trying to photobomb, so I turned the phone at an angle to avoid the annoying girls and took another.

By then, there was loud music playing so we had to more or less shout at each other which was quite exhausting.

'You got a girl back in Bristol?' I just came out with it and I think it took Joe by surprise too.

'Um, no,' he said, 'you?'

'A girl?' I laughed.

'A guy.'

'I don't think I'd be here with you if I had.'

Joe swigged back the rest of his beer then put the glass down on the table and got up, and I took a couple of gulps of the lovely Mojito.

'I really need to find a toilet,' he said, 'be back soon.' I watched him weave around people towards the bar area until he went inside.

People were coming and going with a never ending sea of faces. I sipped up the rest of the Mojito and all that was left was some ice and pieces of mint, so whilst I was waiting for Joe to return, I used the straw to stab at the ice and chop it up. And then I became bored and thinking he'd been gone quite some while, I stood up to see if I could spot him. Oh and that I did.

There he was, the very happy cat chatting quite contently with the same two girls who were getting on my nerves trying to photobomb us when I was trying to take the photo. Some good looking guys started speaking to him and that was that, he'd turned his attentions towards them and it looked like he'd totally forgotten that I'd been waiting for him, on my own, and unable to converse easily with anyone. And there he was all cushy talking Italian with the locals. *That was it*, I said under my breath.

16
Finally

My poor, poor head. Ever since the last time I threw up which was a couple of hours ago my head hadn't stopped pounding. That time was horrible; as soon as I got in and laid down, the whole room went round and round.

And since then, I'd been on top of my bed and still wearing the clothes I had on all day yesterday, except for my sandals. They were over there somewhere near the window splattered with my sick that happened on my way back in the early hours of this morning; alone I might add, thanks to Joe.

The very thought of sick brought that horrid feeling rising up inside me from the pit of my stomach, again. I was breathing really deeply and trying to concentrate on nothing except for not throwing up, when all of a sudden I had to get myself off that bed, with my heart rate at some strange pace, fling the door wide open and hope that nobody was in the one and only bathroom along the hall. Then that weird watery and bitter sensation arrived at the moment I'd slammed the bathroom door shut and wow, up it came again. More pasta and bits. How could there have been any left, I wondered.

If that bidet thing hadn't had been next to the toilet that had its lid down, I don't think I'd have made it in time. I turned on the bidet tap and let the water wash away the stinky mess, but it blocked up the plug hole which meant I had to help it go down by poking it with something. Luckily I could reach for some squirty soap and washed my fingers really well afterwards.

I got up off my knees and hoiked myself up onto the toilet seat and sat there for ages waiting to see if there was some more coming. I prayed there wasn't because my stomach muscles had been pulled so tight, I hurt when I moved and not only that; my head thumped and my throat was sore. But then like some kind of miracle, I actually didn't feel sick anymore. Someone knocked on the door.

'A *momento*,' I called out.

I waited a few moments hoping that whoever it was had gone. I put my ear to the wooden door listening very carefully and decided that as I couldn't hear any sound outside in the hall, it should be safe to leave the bathroom and return to the privacy of my room.

I sat on the side of the bed until I found the effort I needed to go and find the box of Tachipirina and take a couple, and then, after having only been lying on the bed for fifteen minutes, annoyingly, someone was tapping on my door.

'Yes, er, *si*?' I said.

'Caylin it's me, Joe.' *How did you get in*, I thought.

'Go away.'

'I don't want to.'

'Why aren't you still with those girls,' I said, 'or guys.' Hearing myself say that, I thought it sounded a bit childish, but I didn't care.

'I don't want to talk through the door,' he said, 'can I *please* come in?'

'Nope.'

'There's something I want to tell you,' he said, 'please let me in Caylin.'

'What do you want to say, that you're off out with one of those girls or something?'

Joe went all quiet and I was holding my breath to see if I could hear him outside of my door. *I knew it*, I thought.

154

'Caylin, I'm sorry about last night, um, this morning,' he corrected himself. Then I heard him sigh and mutter something like, *this is bloody ridiculous.*

'Last time I'm asking you, please let me in, come on, you're being unreasonable.' *Oh get you*, I thought.

'Nope, you obviously thought you'd found better company last night.'

'If you open the door we can talk about it.'

'No we can't.'

'Why not?'

'Because I've got a headache, I need a shower,' I paused, 'what's the time?'

'Around eleven.'

'Oh.'

'You need to be somewhere?'

'No,' I said, 'look, give me an hour, OK?'

'Sure, see you at twelve then, here,' he said.

'Bye.' I dismissed him just like that.

Oh why did he have to turn up this morning when I was feeling really crappy.

Within forty minutes and with the help of the Tachipirina I'd coped with a shower and I'd even managed to clean up my sandals with some soapy water, which just left enough time for getting dressed and sorting out my face; I was on schedule. Literally just before I'd finished opening the window and tidying the bed, Joe was outside my door again which I then opened.

'Afternoon,' he said smiling at me, 'how's the Mojito head?'

'Shut up,' I said, 'better.'

Joe noticed I was looking at the newspaper he was holding.

'When I was walking past a newsagent this morning, a headline on the board outside made me stop,' he said, 'and so to double-check what I thought I read, I bought this newspaper, look.'

He laid the *Corriere di Siena* newspaper down on my bed.

'You're not going to believe what's happened.'

'Oh.'

On the front page were loads of photos taken yesterday of the Palio and on the right was another headline in bold letters. Joe was running his finger along the printed Italian writing as he was translating the words.

'It says, *young woman hit by taxi, dies,*' Joe read aloud.

We had to turn to another page to read the article.

'Look at this photo.'

He turned the page for me to see the photo a bit better.

'Oh my god, that's Lula, isn't it?'

Only recently I wanted to throw stones at her, or worse, but I hadn't wanted anything *really* bad to happen to her.

'God, it *is* her.' I was more concerned about the girl rather than being angry with Joe any more.

'It says that a witness said he'd recalled shouting to her to watch-out as she stepped into the path of the taxi but obviously she hadn't heard and it was too late.'

'That's terrible,' I said, 'do you think that the ambulance we saw yesterday was the one called to help *her*? The one which was trying to get through the dawdlers?'

I felt gutted.

'We wouldn't know, but it could've been,' he said, 'cause I don't remember hearing any other sirens.'

'Me neither.'

'Seems like the journalist has already found out quite a bit, I'll try to translate it,' he said. 'Basically it tells us that she was Albanian and lived as we already knew, with an Italian. Apparently, she has a brother who is also here somewhere with his wife and young daughter.'

I went to say something when Joe put his hand up, gesturing for me to wait a minute.

'It also says that she allegedly stole money to give to her brother and family to help them live in Italy as they didn't qualify for any assistance from the government,' he said.

'Totally opposite to the help they get back home with all the freebies,' I said. I remembered something Dad had commented on not long ago.

'But now they've voted for the Brexit thing, there could be a lot of changes at the borders, so it might be difficult for foreign people to enter,' I said, 'I'm not really into politics.'

'It's a bit boring, I must admit,' he said before looking back down at the article. He looked thoughtful.

'This journalist couldn't have cared anything about prying into the family business to get all this information; here's a bit more,' he said. 'The brother was supposedly going out to work at various shift times so his wife believed he was earning the money he was taking home. He desperately didn't want his wife to know that he didn't get a job he'd applied for, only his sister knew.'

I interrupted.

'You know, If I think about how the girl was with me, like hiding my All Stars and taking my makeup, it had to be she was envious of me as well as being scared if Vico should dump her for another girl meaning, the risk of losing somewhere herself to live,' I said, 'it figured now why she was all over him.'

'You could be right there.'

'And we heard the other day that Vico didn't go much on the girl's brother,' I said. 'I'm now wondering if he was an arrogant pig to her and used her for *whatever* and she put up with it just so she had a roof over her head.'

I picked up the newspaper and laid on my back holding the paper up to take another look at Lula. The photo must've been a passport or Identity Card photo.

'And all the time she was stealing from him and other people,' I said, 'it wasn't for herself, it was for her brother and his family.'

'And then she goes and gets herself killed,' Joe said, 'wonder what'll happen to them now, perhaps they'll have to go back to Albania.'

I gave a sober nod.

I thought about that family of three and wondered how they'd cope without the girl and the money. I couldn't bring myself to be angry with her any more, not now that she was dead.

'I'd like to do something to help them, but what can I do?'

Joe sighed and shook his head.

'I really don't know, probably not enough for what they could do with.'

'Something is better than nothing,' I said. 'I know, we could go to the taxi people and see if they'd be interested in donating some money.'

'Whoa Caylin, I don't think you should get involved with them,' he said. 'You know, there might be legal stuff going on because of what happened, they might be touchy if they're being blamed for killing her, and it'd be like we're pointing the finger at them too.'

'I didn't think of that.'

'I've seen that people have raised money from something called crowdfunding on the internet,' he said, 'but I think it's only for starting businesses.'

'Hum.'

Then it just happened to come to me, and I was elated with the idea.

'Got it, got it, listen to this.' I sat up cross-legged on the bed next to Joe who at that point was lying on his side.

'Wait 'til you hear this,' I said. 'A sponsored head shave.'

Joe flopped over onto his back.

'A what? No don't worry I heard you.'

'And at the same time, I'll get rid of this black hair,' I said, 'and then I can find a wig similar to my original hair.'

I was so pleased with myself that I'd found the perfect solution.

'There, that's bang-on, we'll raise money for having our heads shaved.'

Joe swung himself round so that he was sitting on the edge of the bed.

'Did you say *our* heads?'

'*Si.*'

'No way.'

'*Si.*'

'Cor, I'd really like to...' and he paused, 'kiss you.'

'You sure? I've been sick.'

'Who cares.'

He turned round and gently pulled me down onto my back, and lying half-on half-off me, he put his lips onto mine. From that moment, I let go of the tiny bit of tension I harboured, and sensing his excited breathing, my eyes closed and I melted into his kiss for such a heavenly long time.

That was the nicest kiss I'd ever had. And how good it was not to feel I was expected to have sex afterwards, although one thing I'd realised, was that I wanted it to be Joe who took my virginity and I knew I was ready for him.

We were cuddled together with my head on his chest of where I could hear his beating heart. I scanned my eyes down towards his trousers where I could hardly miss his arousal, making me feel really giggly and tingly in places.

It was so strange, we both started speaking at exactly the same time.

'Go on, Caylin,' he said, you were first.'

'No, you were.'

'Ladies first.'

'I've forgotten what I was going to say.' That wasn't entirely true.

Joe gave out an anxious laugh, which sounded like he was just about to blurt out something that would ruin everything between us; perhaps he was about to let on about someone back home.

'Caylin,' he said.

Please hurry up and tell me Joe, you're making me nervous, I thought. I kept my head on his chest so he wouldn't be able to see my expression when he broke the news to me.

'Caylin,' he repeated.

You're killing me here Joe, I thought.

'I'm a virgin.'

The moment I heard those words exit his scrumptious lips, I leapt up and bounced around ecstatically on the bed like an absolute loony. I just couldn't believe what he'd just said, I was so relieved that it hadn't been disappointing news and nothing at all what I was expecting. *Thank you*, I thought, *thank you*.

Poor Joe was looking quite worried, so I decided to play him up a bit and stopped still and put on my deadly serious face.

'Joe,' I said. He was peering at me, waiting, and I really was keeping him waiting too, until I couldn't hide my giggles and hold back any longer so I excitedly announced,

'So am I.' He cuddled me into him again and held me tight; I knew he was happy too.

A short while had passed after we'd just laid together; I'd been quite deep in thought and I guessed the same for him.

'Caylin?' he whispered.

'*Si?*'

'What would you say to getting unvirgined?'

Oh my god, this is it, I thought, *this is it, he's asked me, we're going to do it.* And all I could say was,

'I think it'll be OK.' What *was* I saying? It seemed like the barricades were automatically going up. What I should've said was, *what's taken you so long,* or *come here gorgeous.* I really *did* want to do it with him, in that room, there in pretty Siena.

'You sure?' he asked, 'I'm pretty good at waiting, you know.'

'Just joking,' I said, 'course I'm flipping sure, I like you very much.' *Actually, a bit more than like,* I thought.

'Just a sec,' he said softly kissing me on my forehead, and he got up off the bed and went to the window where he pulled the shutters inwards a touch which took away the sun's glare making the room appear much more cosy. Then he went over to the door and turned the lock ensuring there would be no interruptions. Even though I was filled with excitement of the thought that I could soon be losing my virginity to someone I was falling in love with, I couldn't stop myself from being rigid to the spot.

Next, I watched Joe go to a side pocket in his rucksack and saw him pull out a small shiny pack of something and placed it on the little bedside table, I then realised had to be a condom. I wondered if he was as nervous as I was, after all, it was to be his first time too.

Joe was undressed down to his boxer shorts before I'd even contemplated moving myself from where I was sitting. He came over to me and held out his hands enticing me to go to him. You know, it was hard to believe that I'd even planned on how I'd act on this special occasion, and I'd gone over it in my mind time and time again, but yet, I was still pathetically slow on the uptake.

'Come on,' he said gently, 'let's get under the sheet, I want to kiss you again.'

Joe helped me slip my top up and over my head and dropped it onto the chair, then tilting his head to kiss me, he undid and removed my bra, the whole time, I was sensing his excitement. I was down to my pants and feeling quite intoxicated by my rapid heartbeat and the thrill of the unknown. He pulled me strongly to him so my smallish and firm boobs were pressing against his warm chest and whilst we were kissing passionately, we sidled clumsily together onto the bed and slid under the sheet.

I put myself on top of Joe to continue the kiss because he was a good kisser but I was also using it as a delaying tactic. You see, I was scared of how it would be, like if it'd hurt much or if we actually didn't manage it for whatever reason. And I was also scared of spoiling it for him. I didn't want to disappoint.

Then Joe continued to lead the way; he pulled my pants down and we both fiddled with our feet to get my pants down to the bottom of the bed where I gave them a flick with one of my feet, sending them out from under the sheet and onto the floor. And so then we awkwardly repeated this with his boxers until we were underwear-free and I was loving the final freedom on top of him.

'You ready?' he whispered.

'Think so,' I said a little anxiously, 'yes, I am,' I corrected myself giving Joe a warm smile.

He kissed me again on my forehead and moved to sit on the side of the bed reaching for that little shiny packet. He had his back to me so I wasn't entirely sure if he was shaking from nervousness or eagerness whilst he was getting himself ready, but whatever it was, it hadn't deterred him one tiny bit; that I realised when he climbed on top of me fully charged and with one desire in his mind and body: a desire I shared completely.

17

No going back

I don't really know if that was how we'd expected our first time to be. It wasn't the fact that it was our first time together, but our very own first time *ever*.

I know that Joe was trying to be gentle even though he still hurt me, and a couple of times we had to stop because it all seemed so strange and nothing like what Zoe had told me once, but when it finally happened I was dead chuffed that I'd waited until I'd met someone like Joe. And there he was, that very happy cat purring next to me and there we both were; unvirgined.

'Do you mind if I ask you something?'

Joe smiled. 'Feel free.'

'How come you were still a virgin? I mean, by twenty-one I would've thought most guys had done it.'

He traced his finger around my shoulder like he was sketching. 'It's OK,' he said. 'Well, for years my parents had always gone on about stupid boys, their words by the way, who get girls pregnant and since I was a teenager, they'd made it very clear that if I did anything like that, I'd be a disgrace and they'd disown me, shame me even, so basically they scared me into not getting too involved with girls.'

'Cor you poor thing.'

'Yes, well, I think you saw they're quite old fashioned with old attitudes, and anyway, they've never had much time for me; I've been a bit of an inconvenience for them.'

I kissed his chest and cuddled into him.

'But you've had girlfriends, right?'

'A couple,' he said, 'but I kept it as casual as I could, and basically kept myself busy with studying languages and a bit of jogging, etcetera so I didn't have to get too serious with them. Of course they got fed up in the end and went off with guys who were more romantic.'

'And how about you, you've had boyfriends?'

'One or two.' I could tell he was itching to know more.

'Most of the girls in my class aren't virgins anymore,' I said. 'One or two I know didn't wait til they were sixteen and some I heard did it, like the day after their birthdays, but for me, I just hadn't felt ready to do it, not until now.'

'Similar for the guys I think,' he said, 'I remember in school hearing them brag to each other about what they'd done, or with who they did it with.'

'Yeah, the girls who'd done it showed off about it too, and tried to make the rest of us feel inferior,' I said.

'Girls are confusing creatures,' he said, 'one minute you're being snubbed in a coffee bar and the next, it's yahoo.' He was laughing and I knew exactly who he was referring to, so I pinched his skin in a sensitive place around the side of his chest making him wince a bit.

'You know, I'm starving hungry,' he said, 'how about you?'

'Don't think I can face pasta since seeing it again this morning.'

Joe laughed with me.

'How about going to the Conad supermarket, the one near the cinema and getting a sandwich and some fruit, then we could eat in the gardens. What do you think?'

'Sounds cool to me.'

We picked ourselves up some things to eat and drink then crossed the square next to it called Piazza Giacomo Matteotti where on the far side were hundreds of scooters and motorbikes parked in neat lines, I guessed were belonging to the city workers. Then we arrived at another square, Piazza Gramsci which I recognised from having past the other day which was really busy with people getting on and off the buses and coaches.

We were just about to step out and cross over to the gardens when we were compelled to wait to see exactly what was coming along the road. There must have been about six or seven cars speeding through the streets with what looked like a white ribbon flower stuck to their aerials. And the drivers were honking their horns and even the passengers were shouting, but they didn't look like they were trying to warn us of something; more like they were celebrating. Whatever that was about.

Once they'd passed and it was safe to cross, we found ourselves a shaded seat in the gardens. There were other people sitting on seats chatting or eating and others walking through the gardens to the bus stops. If we'd come earlier, we would've been able to look around the open air market, but we were too late, most of the traders were packing away their stuff into their big white vans, and already, some council men were going around cleaning up the paths.

I was still feeling a bit hung-over from the night before, and struggling to eat my sandwich when Joe nudged me.

'Isn't that someone from the pub?' He nodded towards a couple of girls walking in our direction.

'Wasn't one of them talking to the guy with the goatee when you came out?'

'Sure is,' I replied. 'That's Stefania, the one who believed I was a thief, I don't know the other one.' It looked like they'd been buying some things at the market going by the plain flimsy bags they were holding.

There wasn't anywhere I could hide my face behind in time, not that I was afraid of her, I just couldn't be bothered with speaking to her after having felt so humiliated the other night. I could tell that she hadn't noticed me, she was looking towards the horse and military rider statue but she was definitely going to see me sooner or later, as it looked like they were heading to the bus stops which would mean they'd pass where we were sitting.

'Caylin,' she blurted out. I looked directly at her without saying anything, thought I'd let her spit out whatever drivel was going to come.

'I saw the paper this morning, she take the money, not you.'

My stomach turned as she reminded me about the girl I'd completely forgotten about and who was now dead, lying somewhere alone in a morgue. Then I thought about how sad her brother must've been, thinking of his sister who was doing what she could to help him and his family.

'You believed her.'

'Sorry.'

'Me too,' I said, '*arrivederci*.' Then I took another mouthful of water.

Stefania said something I didn't catch and walked away by which time Joe got up off the seat and turned to face me.

'You know, Caylin, she didn't have to apologise to you, but she did.'

'I know that, but you don't understand how I felt having to let them search my bag,' I said, 'it was an unkind thing to do to someone.'

As I said that, I realised I was wrong, poor Joe *would* have known how it felt to be humiliated, and the image popped into my head of him receiving a wallop from that Vico.

'I agree, but she was only doing what she genuinely thought was right, her friends had their money stolen.'

Which then made me think about how I might've reacted if Zoe and Em had had their money stolen, maybe I would've done the same.

'I guess you're right.'

I jumped up off the seat cupping my hands to my mouth and called to Stefania. It seemed like she didn't hear me, maybe she was too far away, well at least I thought she hadn't heard me, unless of course, she'd chosen to ignore me. I called again, but louder. That time she turned to see me waving my arm in the air and beckoning her to come back.

I watched her check her phone, and I think she said something to her friend, then they proceeded to walk back towards us where I greeted her with an apologetic smile which she returned.

'Do you need to catch a bus?'

'Don worry, they pass often,' she said, then she introduced the girl with her.

'This is Chiara.'

'*Ciao*,' me and Joe said at the same time.

'*Ciao*, pleased to meet you.'

'And this is Joe,' I said, 'he's on the same tour as me.'

'Ciao.'

We both shuffled up and gestured for them to sit on the seat next to us.

'Who did that to your eye?' Stefania asked Joe.

'Oh, long story,' he said, and shrugged it off.

I bet she'd spied the blue-green bruise which had now crept below the white gauze.

'Stefania, we know the girl was wrong stealing money, but like we've read in the paper, she had a reason,' I said. Stefania nodded.

167

'I want to help raise some money for her brother and family before we have to leave Siena in a couple of days and we've,' Joe coughed signalling for me to make a correction, '*I've*, had an idea of how to make some money for them.'

'Me and Joe will have all our hair shaved off in public if we can find people to sponsor us, and then the money we raise can go direct to the girl's brother. We've seen the little girl, she's really cute and I bet she'd like some money for toys.'

'I think I understand,' she said.

Joe explained what he could in Italian and I watched her nod in agreement and then she said a few things in return.

'Stefania says that maybe she could help us, but she needs to speak to the people at her club first.'

'*Grazie*,' I said, 'that'll be really cool.'

'Come to find me at the club tonight, near nine o'clock and I hope to tell you something,' she said. 'We have to go, see you soon.'

'Oh Stefania,' I said quickly, 'why were those people in the cars making all that noise?'

'Ah they do that when there is a wedding,' she said, 'also when Italy has won a major football competition, but then it's worse,' she laughed.

'Well, that was pure luck,' I said. 'Just think, we could be a pair of baldies sooner than we think. It'll be a laugh.'

'Let's see, shall we.'

I had to admit that Joe didn't seem too enthusiastic; surely he's seen a lot of men with their hair shaved off, and anyway, it'll grow back quick enough wouldn't it? My fingers were crossed that he wouldn't back out.

We went back to Joe's room and basically lounged around for a while and as he was fortunate to have a small TV in his room, he spent a bit of time switching channels, he said, so that he could listen to the language and see what he was able to understand.

I opened up a box of little chocolate cakes we'd bought from the Conad and removed the cellophane and cardboard holder because I was hoping that one side of it would be plain and was ideal for me to sketch on. I was compelled to sketch Sora to see how she looked without any hair and as she was developing on the cardboard in front of me, I was beginning to feel uneasy and when I'd finally finished, I had to admit it was shocking at how stunningly different she'd become.

Sora was looking directly at me and this time her large green eyes weren't holding back tears of resentment but instead they shone belief in her cause. She was an image of unpretentious beauty. In a way she was reminding me of some of those pretty girls I'd seen in pictures who weren't wearing scarves on their heads, those girls who've had to endure that horrible cancer treatment and had lost their hair; they looked so pure.

'Lookie Joe,' I called his attention holding up my sketch of a bald Sora.

'What an artist you are, she's strikingly beautiful.'

'Yes she is.'

'You OK?'

If the truth were known, no, I was becoming more and more concerned about what Mum and Dad's immediate reaction would be like towards me. In fact, I was dreading it, and couldn't bear to think about it and I was wanting to blank it from my mind until I returned to the hotel in a couple of days time.

'Not really,' I said, 'the tattoo I'm sure I can hide for the time being, so Mum and Dad needn't know about that, but having my head shaved I think will be a massive shock for them.'

'You can always change your mind you know, you don't have to go through with it.'

'But I want to, for that girl's brother,' I said, 'anyway, I've told Stefania now, so I need to do it.'

'Look, I know this is going to sound a bit tough, but you realise it won't be enough to make a difference to their lives, especially if they have to return to their own country.'

'I know that.'

Joe got up off the little chair and stepped over to me, pulling me close to him, giving me a reassuring hug.

'You're a good person, I'm sure things will work out in the end.'

'I hope so.'

I turned my face up towards his and closed my eyes as he reached his lips to mine and keeping our lips together we laid down on his bed to continue the sensational kiss.

We must've fallen asleep cuddled up together having both been sharing an earphone each listening to some of his downloaded music. Joe stretched his legs down along the length of the bed.

'Doesn't it annoy you that your feet stick over the bottom of the bed?'

'I've got used to it,' he sighed.

I wondered if I'd brought up something he didn't like and maybe he could tell from my anxious expression that I wished I hadn't.

'It's OK really, at home we were able to order one longer than the standard length.'

'That's lucky then.'

'Just a bit annoying when I go on holiday or stop over at friends.'

'Hum can imagine, you know, there's a phrase I've heard,' I said, '*people look up to you*, that's a nice phrase isn't it?'

'Ha, better than some I've heard.'

'Yeah, sure,' I said and squeezed his hand.

Before we went out, I checked my phone for messages, there was one from Em and a recorded one from Mum. I listened to Mum's first.

Hello Caylin, Mum here, but I guess you know that. Anyway, wanted to check on how you are and to say that we managed to catch a bit of the horse race on TV. Actually it isn't difficult to catch it, because they seem to be repeating it over and over. What a strange race it was and were you able to see much from where you were? It all looked pretty chaotic if you ask me, and someone said that a girl died after being knocked down by a taxi, how terrible. Oh yes, yesterday morning we were taken to a nice place somewhere in the countryside for a cooking class but Dad didn't want to go to that and be forced to wear a pinny so he stayed by the pool. I learnt how to make ravioli with ricotta cheese and spinach and also tiramisu; did you realise they all make it over here with a lot of raw eggs? I think at first we were all a bit apprehensive about eating it, but it really was scrumptious. That Joe's Mum is a bit strange, she's not really very sociable, she doesn't really say much at all and at the cooking class she hardly spoke to anyone, although she did put filling into the ravioli, I'll give her that. His Dad seems a bit better and what was funny, they were both wearing the exactly the same green T-shirts. I hope that Joe isn't like them and that he's nearby if you need him, he said he wanted to see you were OK. Oh yes, remember the food writer? Well things seem to be warming up between her and the guy with the camera. The other night before we went to bed, Dad and I took a stroll around the gardens when we saw them in the Jacuzzi kissing. I've an idea he's now taking photo's for her article she's supposed to be writing for a national magazine whether much gets done on that. You know, she still insists on wearing those exceptionally thin high heels which she keeps getting stuck in between the flagstones. Can't think of anything else at the mo, so will say ciao and looking forward to seeing you soon. Can you let us know when you're returning to the hotel? Please don't leave it til the last minute, love you. PS. Oh yes, poor Nancy, I can't make out how she feels about it, but there's been an older Italian man turning up at the hotel who we all think has taken a shine to her.

Good job I didn't listen to the message with the speaker on, otherwise Joe might not have been impressed if he'd heard the bit about his parents. I'd better reply but I'll play it safe and do it by text rather than voice so I can't drop myself in it and accidently let on about something I'd rather they didn't know, yet.

Hi Mum, well it's all romance there then! Glad you saw the race. I can imagine what you said about Joe's parents, who aren't really his parents, the woman is his auntie and I don't think either of them have got much time for him. Anyway, he's happy in Siena. No other news except we hired bikes a couple of days ago which was a good laugh. Oh yes, I'll be coming back to the hotel on the twentieth, so in only three days and looking forward to seeing you. Lots of love to you and Dad, Caylin xxx

Just three days.

Hi Cay, a black eye? Can't imagine what's going on over there with you two, for g's sake, come back in one piece please! Oh, Zoe's asked me to say hello to you, and also to ask you if you've given it up to Joe yet, she said you'll know what she means. I know what she means too but wouldn't have quite put it that way. I said I shouldn't ask you, but seeing as she's without her phone and she's a good mate... Anyway, you take your time girl. Speaking of Zoe, she's gone and got herself grounded and phoneless for two days as of yesterday so if she's a good girl, she should be let out and have a phone back tomorrow. She's not allowed visitors but she sneaked a call to me using their house phone. I don't think she'll mind me telling you... she went out with Sarah and Kim to a class disco in a hotel and Zoe and a lot of them got into trouble because they were found skinny dipping in the pool as well as having raided the kitchens. The hotel night reception phoned her Dad, so you can imagine... told me she was going to give a false name so bet she's glad she didn't 'cause if she had... Anyway, got to go, catch ya soon, Em x

Hi Em, sounds like it's all going on there too poor Zoe at least it was only a couple of days, I can't imagine what term I'll get when my parents see me ☹. Anyway, changing the subject, if you get a chance to speak to Zoe you can tell her the answer is maybe yes and maybe no ☺. Oh while I think of it, when you two go out again, ask the barman to make you a Mojito cocktail, but I wouldn't have more than one as it's super nice but super strong. Sorry Em, gotta go now as we're meeting a girl who's sorting something out for us, fill you in when the time's right, Cay xx

We made our way to Stefania's club in time for nine o'clock, and it was then whilst we walked, that I actually realised that my ankle wasn't annoying me for once, and so that was one thing less to worry about.

I couldn't see Stefania but I could see Erica in the distance with some others. It felt a bit strange being back there again and I felt a little awkward having not long ago been branded a thief; I hoped I was doing the right thing and there wasn't going to be some kind of revenge on me. On the other hand, maybe this could be third time lucky, being the third time I'd been there, well at least I hoped it would. Where was Stefania? I wondered.

Me and Joe keeping our eyes open for Stefania to arrive, hung around opposite, near some shops where the staff were preparing to close for the night turning lights out and pulling down some metal shutters.

'Do you think she'll really be here?' I asked.

'Difficult one.'

It was nearly nine thirty and I was starting to feel like a bit of a fool.

'Come on Joe, let's go,' I said, 'it was just a load of tosh and we're obviously wasting our time.'

'Shame, sure you don't want to wait 'til half past at least?'

'Nope.'

I looped my arm around Joe's and disappointed, we turned to walk away in silence, both of us with our own thoughts and dodging others who were out for an evening walk around the city.

I would say it was about ten minutes we'd been walking without saying anything to each other, when we noticed someone's hurried footsteps getting closer from behind making us step into the side of the street and see who was coming. It was Stefania.

'Caylin.' She was out of breath so we had to wait a few moments for her to recover.

'Phew,' she said, 'Erica said she seen you, but you gone by the time I finished to speak with some people. I'm sorry.'

'That's OK,' I said.

'I have good news, a lot of people of my club and their friends said they like your idea and want to watch.'

'Great, but do they understand about sponsoring?' asked Joe.

'Don worry, they know.'

I relaxed a bit.

'We can make it like an event for tomorrow lunchtime, OK?

'An event?' I asked looking anxiously towards Joe. *What kind of event?* I wondered.

'I find someone too who can cut your hair, don worry, it's good.'

'Thank you Stefania, that'll be real cool.'

'See you tomorrow one o'clock at my club OK?'

'Great,' I said, 'fantastic.'

For the second time today we watched Stefania walk away from us, and this time I had giant butterflies in my stomach. She turned round and gave us a wave.

'*A domani,*' she called out.

Me and Joe looked at each other and both of us burst out laughing hysterically. I knew that mine was nervousness; his, I wasn't sure, probably the same.

'Well, you've gone and done it now,' he said, 'there's no going back, they're going to be expecting us tomorrow.'

18

Tre, due, uno

I didn't sleep well at all that night. We were cuddled together in my bed and we were really hot and sweaty even though we only had a light sheet over us. The temperatures had risen again and the night temperature was almost like what we had on a summer's day back in Bristol. I managed to move a bit to give us some air between our bodies.

The trouble was, if we had opened the window, we risked letting in those horrible tiger mosquitoes which were always too small and fast to swat. They were really devious too, the way in which they hid behind something and when you moved it, out they would come and home in on you.

So we were suffering with the heat. In hindsight, we should've stayed at Joe's because his window had a mosquito net you could pull up or down and so we could've had the window open to let the air circulate, albeit warm air. I missed hearing the night crickets too. I remembered lying awake there the other night in Joe's room and hearing a cricket singing outside and thinking how lovely it sounded.

'Are you awake?' I whispered. No answer.

I reached for my phone and checked the time. It was almost five in the morning and still dark so I switched on the phone's light and shone it onto Joe. He looked kind of spooky because his hair and skin looked grey against the white of the sheet in contrast against the eerie dark blue and blackness of the room surrounding us. I noticed that he'd taken off the white gauze at last.

I cheekily moved the light down along his body catching a glimpse of his raised profile beneath the sheet. *No don't*, I thought, *yes, go on*, I dared myself. So I leant out and let my phone slip onto the floor, then followed my hand under the sheet very slowly skimming his chest, down along his stomach and there it was, and there I was a giggly girl waking him up.

'Hey Caylin,' he said stretching himself, 'you ready for some more unvirgining?'

'That'll be telling,' I giggled.

Within a second he'd leapt out of the bed.

'Be right back.'

I knew where he'd gone because I could hear the sounds of his rucksack being moved and I was guessing he was searching for a little shiny packet. I wondered how many he had with him. I quickly huffed into the palm of my hand to see how my breath smelled; it was OK but I wanted to be sure. I remembered that Joe had some toothpaste on the side somewhere so I got out to find it and took a tiny amount to wipe around my teeth; at least I was minty.

Joe was back lying down on the bed before I was, and he'd even been to the window and opened up the shutters. What we could see above a building opposite, the sky was starting to show signs of daylight arriving, and had turned from black to a beautiful indigo colour.

I laid myself on top of him which I knew he loved and kissed him as nicely as I could, before proceeding to move down his chest and pausing just where his pubic hairs started. I couldn't help it, but I hesitated ever so slightly, before continuing to reach the place I knew he'd hoped I'd go and where I stayed for a while. I could tell it was making him very happy. I *wanted* him to be very happy.

I decided to surprise him again and make the next move too, so I reached out for the little shiny packet and took out the greasy smooth condom; the first time ever I'd touched one of those. I could see Joe was watching me with a curious grin as I proceeded to put it on him, luckily without breaking it.

'You ready?' I asked him cheekily.

'You bet.' I didn't think he wanted to wait any longer.

So Joe turned me over onto my back and ever so carefully we made love.

We eventually climbed out of bed after a super lazy lie-in, and by the time we'd showered and sorted ourselves out, it was getting close to the time we'd arranged to meet Stefania at the club. I noticed that Joe had decided to leave the white gauze off his eye as the swelling wasn't quite so bad, but instead, the bruising had become a mystical blend of green and yellow. I wasn't surprised he'd taken it off; I bet it'd annoyed him as I'd seen him have to move his head in a certain direction to see something properly.

It was hot again today and as I didn't have a huge choice of clothes, I'd decided to wear one of the long black skirts with a mint-green strappy top, making me look a bit like a dark mint-crisp chocolate.

I stood for a while in front of the mirror. I hadn't really noticed up to then that I'd got myself a bit of a tan which was fine, except for the freckles I dreaded each summer were starting to show themselves and faintly creeping from one cheek across the bridge of my nose to the other. Joe came up behind me, putting his arms around me and rested his chin on my shoulder.

'Hey gorgeous, we should be going,' he said looking back at me through the mirror.

'Are you nervous?' I asked him.

'Not nervous exactly,' he said, 'just a bit so, so.'

'Me too.'

'You sure you want to go through with it? After all, the girl and her brother wouldn't have known your plan to help them.'

'You want to bottle out?' I asked teasing him.

'Never.'

I wondered if he was telling me the truth.

'Come on, let's do it,' I said, 'Stefania might be waiting.'

Arm in arm we picked our way through the wandering tourists. One time, Joe stopped to read a hand-printed notice in bright colours which was stuck to a post. When I asked him what it was he was reading, he said he didn't understand it. We reached the turning to the street for the club at twelve fifty, when we continued to walk a little slower to survey the situation ahead of us.

'What has she organised?' I said.

'I think we're just about to find out.'

We stood still trying to make out what was happening. The little area used by the club had been taken over with rows of wooden benches where loads of people of all ages were sitting and opposite them there was a small stage area I hadn't noticed before, with two seats on top of it.

'Oh my god,' I said.

'He can't help you.'

'That's not for us, is it?' I was utterly shocked.

'Remember that notice I read...' Joe decided to stop right there as I didn't need to be a science buff to work it out.

'Caylin, Joe.' It was Stefania's voice.

We turned in the direction of where her voice was coming from and there she was, smiling and probably thinking we were

179

two crazy Brits, and extremely relieved we'd turned up. So that was the event idea she'd been conjuring-up.

She came right up to me and gave me a kiss on both cheeks and did the same to Joe.

'Welcome to *your* event,' she said.

'I think it is a good thing you want to give money for to the girl's brother to help them, you are a kind people.'

'Yes, but...' I tried to say something.

'And I want to say sorry to *you*, for thinking you are a *ladro*. This is for to help you to find the money.'

I felt quite overwhelmed at the thought she'd gone and organised the event, and I was thanking my lucky stars that we hadn't bottled-out. We could've so easily had decided not to meet Stefania, unaware that she'd gone to all that trouble. For a moment I lingered on an image of her waiting for us to turn up, and how disappointed she would've been once she'd realised there wasn't going to be any head shaving going on.

'I'm dead chuffed you've done this,' I said. 'What a great idea, *grazie*.'

'I'll second that,' Joe said.

Then, Stefania hit us with another jaw-dropping surprise.

'I spoken to a friend who work in a local TV company and he has organised Paolo to film the event.'

'You mean it'll be shown on TV? I tried my hardest to look very happy about that, and wondered just how Joe was feeling.

'*Certo*, sure,' she said. 'First, Andrea want to interview you, come on.'

I couldn't begin to explain to you how I was feeling on having been thrown literally head first into that situation with less than zero chance of backing out except that I was dead scared and wishing I'd said nothing to her at all. Poor Joe; I doubt he could've believed his ears and all I could do when our eyes met, was pull a stupid oops face at him.

We tagged along behind Stefania and followed her up onto the little stage. I was sweating buckets under my arms which I thought was more from nervousness rather than the heat, so it was a relief that the sun had already passed that area and where we were going to sit was in the shade. Realising that this was going to be recorded and shown on local TV, I had to compose myself which believe me, was going to be a hard task.

There were *sooooo* many people looking right at us, it was terrifying. And Joe, love him, the gentle and quiet person that he was, caught hold of my hand giving it a squeeze, but I wouldn't let his hand go; I wanted him to know I was there for him too. How cruel it was to have dragged him into this with me.

Stefania introduced us to Andrea the journalist, a short man with a dark bushy beard and dark greasy hair, who incidentally spoke English quite well. I was told never to judge a book by its cover.

Everybody hushed when Paolo started filming and Andrea commenced his interview with us. My heart was pounding. All eyes and ears were on us.

'And so, Caylin and Joe, you're from England on oliday and engaged.' I wanted to correct him, but Joe squeezed my hand to warn me not to interrupt him.

'You ave decided to take off all your air to raise money for the family of the girl who died on the day of the Palio, here in Siena.'

'*Si,*' Joe said and I nodded my head. I felt a drip of perspiration trickle down my back.

The journalist repeated the question in Italian for the fascinated audience.

'But there's a little story behind this,' he said, 'that the girl said you were a thief, which we know isn't truth, and made your stay in Siena very difficult.'

I felt as if Joe could read my mind, because I was about to open my mouth and there came the big hand squeeze again. I purposely dug a nail into his palm.

'But it was the girl who was the thief for her brother and is family.'

I'd never been to court, but it certainly felt like I was being scrutinized all right. I raised my hand for permission to speak.

'Yes, she did call me a thief but she was trying to help her family who have no work, and now she's dead,' I said, 'who can help them and their little girl?'

The journalist repeated in Italian what both he and I had said. Then the strangest thing happened, someone started to clap their hands, then another and another until it seemed like the whole of this corner of Siena were applauding us.

'OK, now it's time,' he said, 'who will be the first?'

No way should I make Joe go first, even though the thought was very appealing.

'Me,' I called out with my hand raised again.

'You sure?' Joe whispered.

'Course.'

The audience were being joined by onlookers who were passing by, and by that time there was a huge buzz of voices echoing off the tall ancient buildings. A pretty woman called Elisa with dyed blond hair was introduced, apparently from a Siena hairdressers who had agreed to shave off all our hair for nothing; of course, she got free publicity for her salon so she'd have been stupid not to have done it. Elisa draped a blue shoulder cape around me, her perfectly manicured and brightly painted red nails fastening it with the Velcro. Her tanned hands looked shiny like she'd just applied some hand cream, but it was easy to tell that she was over forty from the sticking out veins the same like my lovely mum has. What will you think, Mum?

I wondered. Some Italian pop music started coming out from tinny sounding speakers somewhere. *Here we go*, I thought.

A couple more drips of perspiration ran down my back. She plugged the cutters into the adapter attached to an electrical lead brought outside from a building and switched them on. Her hands tilted my head and I shut my eyes. The whirring noise got close until I felt the cutters make contact with my hair, her hands tilting my head one way then another as she stripped my hair away. I could tell that she smoked and I wished she didn't because every time she got real close to me I could smell her stale and stinky breath. Who'd want to kiss her? I wondered, only another smoker I supposed.

I felt hair fall onto my free hand which was resting on my lap. Joe was holding my other hand. Elisa's hand guided my chin upwards where I finally opened my eyes to be reminded that all those people were staring right at me. I turned to Joe.

'What's it like, Joe?'

'Beautiful.'

I really hoped he was being honest.

Apparently Elisa hadn't quite finished; next she brushed some kind of nice-smelling foam all over my head and then we went through the phase of head tilting again, and I was reminded to keep perfectly still whilst she used a sharp razor to do a closer shave until my head was completely smooth. How strangely nude I felt when wisps of air skimmed my scalp. I wondered if she knew that my hair was originally red and not the dyed jet black that was strewn everywhere.

Now and then when my head had been tilted, I was able to look downwards at the stage, where I'd caught a glimpse of Elisa's legs and feet. At the end of her three-quarter length blue leggings were her tanned stick-like legs poking out finishing with a pair of very sparkly high-heeled sandals and pedicured toenails. It seemed like she hadn't missed a thing. The whole scene was like a great big entertainment show and all the while, the journalist commentated in Italian to the audience and the camera.

In a way I wished I'd known that it was going to be like this, at least I would've had a chance to make sure I had paid more attention to my makeup. But on the other hand, if I'd known, maybe I would've been too much of a chicken and bottled out all together.

Her final thing was to use a soft brush all over my face and neck to rid all the remaining hair, and removed the shoulder cape away from my sticky and sweaty back. Still sitting, I turned towards Joe who gave me a lovely grin and leant over and hugged me, which seemed to encourage the audience to clap very enthusiastically again.

That was one of the longest fifteen minutes I'd ever spent, but it was finally over for me, except I still had to wait for the moment until I was allowed to see myself in a mirror. I sat back on my chair and ran my hand all over my head giving myself excited giggles which I couldn't hide from the audience.

And so it was Joe's turn and I held his hand for reassurance just as he did for me, only this time, I was able to see exactly how it was done. Elisa waited holding the cutters poised to start on Joe whilst her assistant hurriedly got up onto the stage and swept my hair away.

His eyes were closed, maybe not as tightly shut as I'd had mine and I could see he had some beads of perspiration above his top lip. I watched mesmerised by Joe's striking bone contours as Elisa tilted his head one way, then another, until all his blond locks had been destroyed. I wondered how she imagined Joe got his colourful bruising and luckily, nobody had asked. There was a slight pause between the cutting and the foam being smeared onto his bald head when he turned towards me.

'Go on then,' he said.

'Drop-dead gorgeous.'

'Yeah, right.'

The journalist was really kidding around with the audience and getting them to clap their hands to the music's rhythm when Elisa, obviously in the mood for jigging around had managed to snick Joe's skin behind his ear. He flinched and put his hand to the place to discover he was bleeding. The assistant passed him some tissue to dab it, and I noticed from that moment, Elisa in her sparkly sandals didn't dare gyrate around him anymore. She couldn't run the risk of nobody wanting to book shaves with her if she happened to snick skin.

Elisa had finally finished moving around Joe's head with that *extremely* sharp blade when the moment came for the assistant to carry a tall mirror onto the stage for us to see ourselves bald for the very first time.

The journalist had got the audience clapping in time together and as I was the first to be shaved, I had the pleasure of looking first in the mirror. *Tre, due, uno*, they all shouted, and the mirror was spun around in front of me. And all I could do was let out a hysterical scream and the audience responded with cheers. Joe managed to calm me down with a cuddle so that my scream was reduced to uncontrollable laughter; never, had I imagined seeing myself bald.

When it was Joe's turn, I could stand with him and on the count of *tre, due, uno*, the audience shouted for the last time before the mirror was turned round. Fortunately, his reaction was less frenetic than mine although he was laughing a lot. I didn't know if he did it for the filming, but he picked me up off my feet and spun me round and round, his lips pressed firmly on mine.

The journalist signalled for us to sit back down once more before he started speaking again over the microphone.

'OK, money has been given from the kind people here and also from other people who hear about your help to the family.'

He plunged the microphone in front of me as he translated what he'd said into Italian.

'Er,' I said, '*grazie*, we hope that it will help them with something or they can buy something they need for their daughter.'

'Sure they will,' he said, 'because up to now, the total has reach three thousand two hundred euro, *and* there will be more from people who watch your event on TV later *oggi*, sorry, today.'

'Wow,' I said, '*grazie* very much.' I couldn't think of anything else to say. Then out of the blue, Joe amazed me with his courage in taking hold of the microphone and pulled me to stand up with him in front of all those people.

'What I want to say to you all, is that I have only known Caylin for a short time, and during that time, I've learnt that she is a unique person and she has a heart of gold,' he said. I gave him a friendly thump for that. And then he went and repeated it in Italian which I could see he had totally knocked the pants off everyone.

'*Bravi*,' they shouted to us, '*Bravi*.'

19

Butterflies

That was a lunchtime experience I shan't forget for a long time. The cameraman, journalist and hairdresser and most of the people left quite quickly, no doubt hungry the same as I was.

Stefania said that they should have all the money raised in time for tomorrow morning, which was truly lucky as the day after, we had to leave Siena to return to the hotel and I didn't want to miss seeing the family's surprise. I really hoped that they'd be home when we knocked on their door.

I guessed it must've looked strange passing by a couple of people with their heads shaved, because the number of people or children I caught looking at us were many, and if I'd turned to look behind, there was always someone looking back at us. But it didn't really bother me; I felt a sense of satisfaction that I, I was speaking for myself, had finally done something to help someone even though the amount might not come to very much or might not help them a great deal.

I'd seen different fundraising events going on in Bristol, but I'd never had the opportunity to take part, either because I was too young or because I wasn't able to for reasons like, a fun run which was actually a marathon run and too far for normal people.

'The only channel I can find is this one,' Joe said.

He was flicking through all the channels on his TV, whilst I was trying to find the right pose to do a selfie to send to Zoe and Em.

'It has to be this one which she said, Siena TV.'

'Sound's familiar, let's leave it switched on, and see if they show local news on that one,' I replied.

It was four forty-five in the afternoon and I didn't want to go anywhere until we'd seen the news; I didn't want to miss *us* on TV and I was feeling super nervous.

'Wait a minute,' he said, 'the TV menu says there should be news at five o'clock.'

He adjusted the shutters so that the light didn't interfere with the screen, before cuddling up next to me on the edge of the bed where we stared at the screen together in anticipation. I felt a bit conscious that the volume was high enough that anyone passing below could have heard it and I knew that Dad would have told me to turn it down long ago. I just didn't want to miss *anything*.

We both sat really quiet, just waiting whilst my poor stomach did summersaults. And then it came on the screen, *Siena TV Notizie*.

'Oh my god,' I said, 'it's coming.'

And there we were on the stage, from the start to the finish, me laughing hysterically, Joe speaking in Italian, and us two baldies in front of all those people and all the others who were watching the news. *Was that really us?* I wondered.

'Can't be,' Joe said, 'I don't know if I just heard the presenter say how much has been raised so far, I think he said just over four thousand euros.'

'Cor,' I said.

'Like, triple wow,' Joe said.

The news programme ended, and using the remote, Joe found a music channel to put on.

'Do you think we should rub some sort of oil on our heads?' he asked peering into the mirror.

'I think so, and also, we have to be careful with the sun you know.'

'Look, I found this moisturising lotion in the drawer when I first booked into this room,' he said flipping the lid up to take a smell. I took a sniff of it.

'Umm, smells nice,' I said, 'come here you lovely bald person.' I pulled him over to the bed, sitting him down where I knelt up behind him.

I squeezed a little of the lotion in the palm of my left hand and proceeded to massage Joe's soft head very gently, round and round. I could just about spy his reflection in the TV screen; I was sure he had his eyes closed.

'Right, that's it,' he said, 'let's swap.'

I was a bit shocked at his sudden change.

'Didn't you like it?' I thought I'd done something wrong.

'Too much.'

'Oh.'

It was his turn to be kneeling behind me, so I shut my eyes enjoying my head massage when after a few moments, his warm moisturised hands slipped down my shoulders and continued down inside my top. How wonderful that felt, and how exciting it was to feel his bulge that he was pressing into my back.

'Fancy making sure you're no longer a virgin?'

'That's for me to know and you to find out,' I replied in a naughty tone.

This afternoon we did lots of different things to each other, things I guessed all couples did behind closed doors in private, once we'd finished kissing that was. I'd never felt so aroused, and today was the very first time that someone had given me an orgasm. Joe took me to paradise and back and Joe was a very happy cat again.

I was trying to get over the fact of how mega weird my skin felt against the pillow whilst we were lying together on our backs with the single sheet over the top of us.

'Joe?' I said, there was no answer.

'Joe?'

'Sorry, I must've been drifting off.'

'Would it be OK with you if I took a selfie of us here together like this, just our heads and shoulders?'

I didn't really give him a chance to answer me.

'I'd like to send it to Zoe and Em to show them our new hair styles,' I said, 'would that be OK by you? Oh go on, pretty please.'

'If you must, no more OK?'

'Course not,' I said, 'smile.'

There wasn't any need to check in the mirror how my hair looked before a selfie.

Hey guys, going to send you a selfie of me and Joe with the next message, (hope you've behaved yourself Zoe and got your phone back) best if you sit down first Em, before opening it OK?! ☺

Message sent, now for the photo.

Girls like to have fun]

And sent. Poor Em, I'd like to be a fly on the wall when she opened it.

Today was one of the weirdest days of my life. Joe and I went out into the city to eat at a pizzeria and every now and then, we were interrupted with apologies from various people, because they wanted to hand us some euros to add to the collection. They'd told Joe that they'd seen the event on the local news.

But the weirdest thing was later, when we were eating ice cream sitting on the tiny wall of the fountain in Piazza del

Campo. It was only the *B......* Vico, who was coming up to us and he had that other guy from the apartment with him too. My stomach turned.

'Have you seen who's coming our way?' I said. 'Look to your left, past the couple of families with pushchairs.'

'Hold this please.'

Joe immediately handed me his ice cream and stood up waiting for them to get closer and I thought he looked like he was preparing to defend himself; but then I didn't think so. Instead, he had a karate style stance and clenched fists; he was ready to attack Vico.

I really didn't want Joe to get hurt again; I didn't even want him to fight. I'd seen too much of that back home. Couldn't people talk it out anymore? I stood up close to Joe, my heart was pounding.

'Joe, please.' My voice was shaky.

He wasn't saying anything, just staring straight at Vico and his mate. I felt so terrible for him seeing those two blokes heading towards us. I didn't know what to do. I couldn't help it, but my eyes pricked with tears I was so afraid of what they were going to do to him. Then Vico put his hand out in front of himself like he was signalling for Joe to keep calm. I looked at Joe and it seemed like he'd decided that he wasn't going to fall for anything. He was keeping the same stance and silently surveying the situation we were in.

Vico and his mate stopped a couple of metres away from us and I couldn't bet my life on it, but as I was able to see them a bit closer, there didn't seem to be any malicious expression on their faces.

Vico started speaking in Italian to Joe who was still poised ready for a counter-attack. It was obvious he wasn't going to let his guard down all the while he listened to what Vico had to say to him. Vico continued speaking when I realised that his voice sounded remorseful, his expression was remarkably different to that of the other day outside of his apartment; it was one of deep regret, I didn't think for what he'd done to Joe, I was sure it was for Lula who'd lived with him and whom he'd never see again. I was trying to feel sorry for him.

Joe adjusted himself into a more tranquil posture and after a few seconds, I assumed where he was gathering his words, he began responding in Italian. Vico then said something else with a touch of friendliness in his eyes, stepped forward and held out his right hand to shake Joe's. Only then I'd realised that whilst I was so intent on what was happening, the two half-eaten ice creams I was holding had been dripping down my hands and onto the ground.

Vico put his right hand into his jeans back pocket, producing a sealed envelope and whilst saying something, handed it directly to Joe who then turned to me.

'He said he saw us in the square and went home to get this,' Joe said. 'There is a thousand euros inside this envelope for you to add anonymously to the rest of the money raised for the girl's family. He's made it absolutely clear that he doesn't want the family to know it's come from him.'

Well I wasn't expecting an envelope full of dosh, let alone from him.

'*Grazie* Vico,' I said.

'Joe, please can you say this to Vico for me,' I said. 'Even though I hate him for what he did to you, deep down he is a good person, he helped me get to Siena and now he's helping that family, also that I'm very sorry about what happened to his girlfriend.' I didn't know what else to say, so I left that to Joe.

At the end of our surprise meeting in the busy and moonlit Piazza del Campo, Vico and his friend shook both our hands and walked soberly away in the direction of which they came. I was gobsmacked.

'Wow.'

I wanted to jump and shout at the thought of another thousand euros as well as what people had given us already that evening which we hadn't yet counted.

I found a bin and threw away the messy ice cream cones and went back to join Joe where I looped my arm with his and we strolled out of the square.

'Apparently Vico and the girl's family had fallen out some time ago,' he said, 'he didn't say what it was about, but he said that he prefers to leave the situation like it is.'

'But surely if they knew that a lot of the money came from Vico, they'd make up, you know, build bridges.'

'No.' Joe said firmly.

'We can't say anything, we can't do that. We don't know what went on, so it might not be as simple as that, and I've said we'd give his money anonymously like he's asked.'

'I might not totally agree with you, but I see your point,' I said.

We continued walking along arm in arm together through the lantern-lit streets without saying anything else, both of us alone with our own melancholic thoughts.

In my room, Joe poured coins and notes out of his trouser pockets onto the bedside table.

'Look at this.' Under the warm coloured light of the table lamp shone heaps of euro coins and notes.

'It's a good job we're honest people,' I said.

'What do you mean?'

'Well, it would be so easy not to put this money into the collection.'

Joe glared at me; it was a look I'd never seen come from him before.

'Yeah, right.'

'Only joking!' And I was, honestly.

There had to be something like a hundred or two hundred euros, who knows, except it was an amazing sight. Joe scooped the lot into the bedside table drawer.

'We can count it all tomorrow.'

I hadn't noticed again that I'd received some messages during the evening and there was also a voice recording from Dad which put me on edge straight away. Joe was trying to tune in to a radio station on his phone, so I laid on the bed making myself comfy before I looked at the messages. I wanted to open the messages I could see had arrived from Zoe and Em first, but I was drawn to listen to Dad's before anything else otherwise not knowing what he was saying would haunt me right up to the time I pressed the *play* button.

Caylin, Dad here. I heard him breathe in and then breathe out with a sigh. Oh, big, giant butterflies. *Someone in the group said we should watch the Siena news this evening, which sure enough your mum and I did along with probably nearly all of the hotel's guests.* I was starting to feel sick, of course there was no doubt what they'd seen. *We're both stunned and don't quite know what to say to you at the moment, but be sure that when we see you the day after tomorrow, we shall be looking forward to speaking to you. Dad.*

I put my phone down next to me and just laid there staring up at the white ceiling. Could they have also seen my mouldy tattoo? The day after tomorrow will be the worst ever day of my life. In the background of my thoughts was an Italian TV programme presenter spouting off about something or another and really getting on my nerves.

'You OK?'

'Nope.'

Joe moved closer to me and gave me a kiss on my stupid bald head.

I wiped his kiss off my head and after feeling my strange and warm scalp, I screamed at him.

'Don't do that!'

And I turned over onto my stomach squeezing the pillow onto the top of my head to hide myself. Joe didn't respond except he too sighed, just like my Dad had, and then he sat there and rubbed my shoulders whilst I cried for ages and ages. I think he'd guessed I'd heard from my parents.

'Come on, Caylin,' he said, 'it'll all work out fine, I'm positive of that.'

'You don't know my dad.' I said from underneath the pillow.

'No, but don't forget we're in this together, I'm right by your side.'

Hearing Joe say those words lifted my distressed spirits.

'But aren't *you* worried about what your parents will say?'

'Not that much,' he said, 'besides it's not forever.'

He had a point there.

'Have you heard from your friends?'

That prompted me to pull myself together and sit up on the bed. Joe went and got me some tissue from the bathroom so I could blow my nose. My eyes felt so sore and puffy and I truly hoped they would've calmed down by tomorrow morning when we go to see the girl's brother and family.

'Let's look together,' I said whilst moving over a bit so Joe could sit next to me with our backs against the wall.

'I'll open Em's first as I think she'll be the one who'll be the most depressing.'

Cay, it had to be a bet, right? All that beautiful long, auburn hair, given up first for black gothic and now, bald? Sure you've not been smoking something? And that Joe, is he some kind of bad influence on you?? ☹ Looking forward to seeing you in a few days and hopefully without anything else done to yourself, Em x PS. How am I going to stop Zoe now???

'Told you about Em, didn't I? She's the worrier.'

'Not a bad thing really, if she helps to keep you under control.'

I walloped him on his thigh and must've caught him just right to accidently give him a dead leg.

'Now for Zoe's message.'

Oh Cayeee, what're u like! ☺ Actually, no need 2 answer...Big question coming, WHY?...no frizzy hair days 4u4 a while then... lookin cool 2gether, u naughty pair! Maybe we can make it a 3some (not in that way ☺☺), I mean without hair LOL, but that'll leave dear Em out, so best not. Catch u soon in person, Ciao Zoeeeee xx

'Poor Em, seems like she's got a busy life trying to keep both of you in check.'

Yes, in reality that was very true, bless her.

I couldn't see that I'd received any message at all from Mum. Butterflies.

20

Cake with aliens

I woke up to our last whole day here in Siena.

That's strange, I thought, where had Joe gone? I'd put my arm around behind myself and his part of the bed was cool, not warm as usual from our body heat. I turned over and looked around the room. Perhaps he'd gone to the bathroom. No, that wasn't it, his shoes had gone.

I checked the time on my phone, it was only eight fifteen, so why had he gone out? I got up out of bed and opened the window to push back the shutter. I would've loved to have climbed back into bed and wait for Joe to get back, but maybe I'd have to wait too long, then it'd be a rush to get out and meet Stefania and the journalist. I decided to go and have a shower.

Weird or what. I stood underneath the shower and automatically put my hands up to run my fingers through my hair to help the water get to where it was meant to, but it actually scared me to have my hair missing for the first time under the shower. I was sure I could remember hearing someone say at the hairdressers back home, that you should continue to use shampoo because every day there would be a little bit of hair growth.

So I tipped a tiny bit of shampoo into the palm of my hand and after I'd worked it into a lather, I pretended to wash my hair which was well weird, and making me giggle out loud. Drying was great, because there was nothing to dry.

After I'd tidied up most of the watery mess in the bathroom I went back to my room where I didn't remember having had left the door open a smidge. I let out a sigh of relief when I realised it was Joe inside the room.

'Hey Caylin, look at today's newspaper headline that's outside the newsagents.'

He'd taken a photo of it and found it on his phone to show me.

'It basically translates as,' he said, 'couple, have heads shaved and raise at least five thousand euros for family of dead girl.'

Before I could say anything, he added,

'And look at the newspaper,' he said, 'ta da.'

There we were on the front cover and there was an article on page seven all about what we'd done. I took a photo of the two pages so I could send it to the girls back home not for any reason other than to help explain *why*.

Hey guys, apols this is going to be a short message; next two photos will help explain even though it's in Italian. Long story but good reason. Will tell you all when I get back, but now we have to go out and I'm nervous as hell about seeing Mum and Dad tomorrow, Cay xx

'Let's count how much money was given to us last night,' I said eagerly because I just couldn't get over how people who recognised us from the TV, literally handed their money over. I patted the bed to encourage Joe to sit between me and the bedside table. He pulled out the little drawer and tipped the coins and notes out onto the top and he also opened up Vico's envelope.

Joe added up the money, then I recounted just because I like counting money and flicking the coins off the top into my cupped left hand and making small piles coming to ten euros and even one euro piles with the coppers. I'd formed loads of little neat stacks, finally adding those up as well as the notes.

'Go on then,' he said, 'what do you make it?'

'Er, well I think it's, one thousand, three hundred and thirty-six euros, eighty-two cents,' I said, 'I think.'

'Hum,' he said sighing, 'I made it, one thousand, three hundred and thirty-five euros, eighty cents.'

I laughed and sighed at the same time and suggested we counted together.

'Right then, one thousand, three hundred and thirty-seven euros, eighty-two cents, that's it,' we both agreed.

'Wow, that's brill,' he said.

'Yeah and wait til we add it to what was given at the event yesterday,' I replied.

We gathered the dosh and found a small plastic bag to put it in and got ready to go and meet Stefania and the journalist.

'Didn't she say we're to meet her at that bank, Monti something in the street behind the Piazza del Campo?' I asked.

'Yikes, it's nearly eleven now, we've got to go or we'll be late', he said, 'yes there.'

We hurried along the streets together and apologising to groups of Japanese tourists we were having to push our way through, as we didn't want to be late. I wouldn't have normally cared about having to dodge the wanderers, but this morning it was imperative we were on time and the Japs were really annoying me with their gigantic cameras hanging around their necks and carrying their tinsy umbrellas to keep the sun off their pale skin.

'There's the bank,' I said, 'what's the time?'

'Don't know, let's just get there.'

We arrived breathless and sweating and stepped inside the doorway near the bancomat machine away from the crowds and sun. I'd never been inside of an Italian bank before and so we peered in through the huge dark tinted windows. It was ten past eleven meaning we were ten minutes late and I could see Stefania and the journalist were sitting down in where it appeared to be a waiting area; I guessed they were waiting for us to turn up.

The bank seemed to be really hot on their security. I pushed the door to enter but it was locked. I pushed it again and heard a click when the door unlocked and we could go inside something resembling a big glass cubicle. Then, we had to do the same process through another door until we were finally permitted inside the bank.

Stefania and the journalist greeted us with big smiles as we went over to join them, where I accidently kicked his camera which he'd stupidly left on the floor and naturally I cringed but he told me not to worry.

'You will be very appy', the journalist said, 'when you know how much euros there are.'

'In fact,' I said looking at what I'd written down, 'we have one thousand, three hundred and thirty-seven euros, eighty-two cents to put in too.' I was so excited, I didn't give him a chance to say the amount they'd collected from yesterday.

'Wait for the total,' he smiled.

The journalist took the money from us and went over to queue to speak to a person sitting behind a wooden counter. After around fifteen minutes, he returned with a slip of paper which he showed all of us, where we could quite plainly read that the grand total was an awesome six thousand, five hundred and ninety-one euros, thirty-three cents. I think we were all completely speechless.

They said that the money was safer in the bank and it would be available when the brother needed it, and even if there were still people who wanted to donate, they could still do that at the bank. They gave us a special piece of paper where the grand total so far was written in massive fancy numbers which we could present to the brother. You couldn't imagine how happy I was and truly hoped he'd be at home.

We all left the bank through another set of double doors for which we then had to wait for a green light to allow us to leave. Stefania and the journalist didn't know precisely where the family lived, so they had to follow me and Joe to the place where we originally saw the girl's brother and family. And the easiest way for us to remember, was to retrace our footsteps back to the alleyway.

So there we were again, this time four of us, weaving in and out between the Japanese and sometimes American tourists until finally we were at the entrance to the little slippery alleyway. What would we do if they weren't home? I was starting to feel apprehensive.

Thankfully, having reached the bottom of that stinky old lane, we were back out in the warmth of the sun and from where we were, I could see the door of where we had to knock.

'It's just over there,' I said pointing in the direction. I'd been hoping that as it was coming up to lunchtime, maybe there was a bigger chance that they'd be home, but it all seemed so quiet.

Me and Joe stood a little bit back from Stefania and the journalist when the journalist used his right thumb to press the door buzzer. I wanted to look really happy but it was difficult because I felt anxious and wondered how they'd react. After all, his sister had just died and maybe they wouldn't have wanted our smiling faces and a journalist on their doorstep at such a terrible time. Maybe they wouldn't want to accept charity. I was having second thoughts and wondered if it wasn't such a good idea and then it was too late, I heard a woman's voice come through the speaker.

The journalist put his face near to the speaker underneath the buzzer and said a few things to it including the mention of mine and Joe's names, for which the voice said something back, followed by a click as if she'd hung up a phone and cut us off. Then came another click which unlocked the outside door, and the journalist turned round sticking his thumb up signalling to us that all was good. I hadn't realised up to then, that I'd been holding my breath in anxiety, and letting it out was such a relief.

'Come on,' he said, ' we can go up.'

We followed Stefania and the journalist up the dark stairs to be met by the wife who said her name was Ariana as she welcomed us all into her small and cosy kitchen-diner. It was possible to hear a man's and child's voice in another room and within a few moments, a door opened and they entered the lounge also. Now that we were quite close to the man, it was easy to see that he was the brother of the dead girl; they both had the same shape and colour blue eyes. Even the little girl's eyes, her niece had the same resemblance.

Ariana introduced her husband as Besmir and the little girl was called Nevena. We all shook hands briefly and we were invited to sit down. Fortunately, there were just enough places; four wooden chairs around the square wooden table and there was a settee where me, Joe and Stefania could sit. Little Nevena wanted to sit on her daddy's lap and I noticed that she wouldn't look at me and Joe.

I thought that Besmir had probably sussed why we were all there, especially as photos of me and Joe being hairless had been plastered everywhere, and there we were, sitting on their settee inside their home. Then I wondered that maybe they hadn't seen the Siena TV news or the newspapers, and they'd no idea about any of it.

The journalist spoke before anyone else with a kind manner, and even though I hadn't had a clue what he was actually saying, I could sense that when he was speaking he was thinking about the words he was using for such a sensitive subject. I was studying the expressions on their faces and I didn't think they knew anything at all about the money raising event. It was a complete surprise. The journalist presented the slip of paper from the bank where they could clearly see the amount of money.

I saw Besmir stretch out his left hand to squeeze Ariana's hand she was resting on the table, he had tears in his eyes and as I was watching those tears overflow and run down his cheeks, I couldn't stop myself from crying too.

'I'm sorry,' I said rummaging around in my bag for a tissue. Thankfully Stefania found one quicker than I had, and passed it to me where I blotted my eyes and tried to pull myself together. I hated myself for crying; I didn't even know those people and I must've looked pathetic. The last thing they needed was some emotional seventeen year old snivelling in their home. Joe pulled me closer to him and whispered *don't worry* in my ear.

Then the atmosphere completely changed with Ariana, in a stern voice, saying something to Besmir and he was banging his hand on the table. I didn't think any of us really expected that and all we could do was sit quiet and hoped they'd calm down. That was a horrible couple of minutes.

Besmir was speaking through his tears and Ariana also crying, was patting little Nevena's back as she tensely clung to her daddy with her head burying into his shoulder. I desperately wanted to know what he was saying especially about his sister who he kept glancing over to the mantelpiece where there was a photo of her. I could also see another photo which to me looked like them both as children with who must've been their parents on a farm or somewhere in their own country because there were some chickens in the background.

Ariana seemed to relax and regain her calmness and went over to the worktop and brought some cake over to the table which looked home-made, some plates, serviettes, bottles of water and glasses. She cut slices and passed the plates around and poured the water out. It was a huge relief she'd done this because that gesture finally put us all a bit more at ease and the tears stopped, maybe just for a while at least.

Whilst the journalist chatted to the family, Stefania turned to me and Joe.

'They are so happy for the money,' she said, 'they can now pay to take the sister's body and have the funeral in Albania, they country.'

'Oh,' I said. I wasn't expecting Stefania to tell me that.

'Where is that near?' I asked, geography had never been one of my stronger points.

'Just up from Greece I think,' Joe said.

'Oh yeah, you're right.' I pretended I knew.

And just like that, a really strange fact just popped into my mind that I actually remembered a teacher having told us once. Apparently, if Albanian people nodded their head it meant they didn't agree with you and if they shook their head it meant they did; weird. I decided to try to forget that fact for now, otherwise there was a massive chance I'd be utterly confused on what was going on.

'Will they move back to Albania?' I asked.

'If he can't get a work,' she said, 'and Ariana now know that he has no work.'

Well that made sense why they suddenly began arguing; the article the journalist had in his hand spoke about the sister stealing for them.

'They can speak Italian,' I said.

'Albania is only across the sea from Italia and the people can watch Italian TV and listen to the radio.'

'Oh.'

The journalist turned to speak to us from his chair at the table.

'The family are happy to ave a photo with the bank's slip of paper with Caylin and Joe, come.'

'I'd like Stefania in the photo too because she organised everything,' I said.

'But it is your idea,' she responded.

'Come on Stef.'

So me and Stefania stood on one side next to Ariana, and Joe was on the other side next to Besmir, and somehow they'd managed to persuade little Nevena to stand in the middle of us all at the front. I had the feeling that she still wouldn't look at me and Joe, I guessed to her, we looked like a pair of aliens.

The journalist had taken two or three photos *for safety* he said, and he needed to go home soon so he could write the piece for the newspaper in time for tomorrow. I took a sneaky peek at my phone and saw that in fact it was almost one thirty; and washing my alien head this morning seemed yonks ago.

It felt like a happy-sad goodbye when we prepared ourselves to leave their home. Happy because maybe we'd helped them a bit, but sad for their situation and I've always been useless at goodbyes especially if I knew it was a farewell goodbye. Both Ariana and Besmir took it in turns to give me, Joe and Stefania very strong hugs where I noticed again that Besmir had tears coming, and you know, so did I.

When Stefania suggested that me and Joe went out with her and some friends for our last night in Siena, I assumed that it would be only with Erica and co., but I'd assumed wrong. She'd said they'd meet us at Dino's Trattoria and by chance, having spotted the funny green car thing with the restaurant stickers all over it parked outside on the hill, we found it just in time for eight o'clock. But when we entered inside, we were confronted with a noisy sea of faces and it was *that* nerve-racking I wanted to turn and leave. It seemed like everyone was looking at us from all directions, from the tables up on the right, ahead of us and through to the left.

Joe nudged me and was nodding in the direction of Stefania who I saw was coming towards us from a table she'd been sitting at further back towards a cabinet with oils and vinegars. And when she reached us, she turned to everyone and basically announced us as if we were celebrities. All that cheering and clapping was sooooo unnecessary and even some people dining who looked like tourists were joining in the occasion too. It wasn't like we'd saved someone's life or stopped world war three from happening; we'd only had our heads shaved, and like Joe had said, it wasn't forever. It was nothing compared to what some people did for others.

'Come on,' she said, 'tonight is for you.'

Although I was speechless, I still managed to give her a hug and kissed her on her cheek.

'Ah, but we wouldn't have been able to do any of it without you.'

We followed Stefania to her table where there were two reserved chairs and immediately we were asked to choose what we wanted to eat from the menu as most had already ordered and their dishes were being brought out from the kitchens.

'You didn't need to do this, Stef,' I said in between crunchy mouthfuls of toasted bread with tomato and basil.

'I also wanted you to know I'm very sorry for the other night,' she replied.

'It doesn't matter,' Joe said, 'you're forgiven.'

'I'll drink to that,' I added taking a large slurp of Peroni beer.

'Hey,' he said, 'go steady, remember?'

'Yes, Dad,' I joked. Then that horrible feeling swept over me which wasn't the alcohol. I suddenly thought about tomorrow and seeing Mum and Dad. It was going to be terrible.

'You OK?' Stefania asked me looking quite concerned. I exhaled and relaxed the grip I had on the beer glass I was holding, telling myself to blank tomorrow out of my mind until tomorrow comes.

'Sure, I'm fine.'

There was loads of chitchat going on, some of her friends were trying really hard to practice speaking in English and Joe was using every opportunity he could to improve his knowledge of the Italian language, during which time, we ate way too much. The dish of gnocchi with meat sauce was super scrummy and I managed to get Joe to trade a piece of his delicious whacking big steak for some of them. Then I polished off a creamy Panna Cotta pud and still had room to help Joe with his sickly Profiteroles. I was absolutely beaten and stuffed.

It was strange to think that if we hadn't been in the gardens a couple of days ago at the same time as Stefania, we'd probably had never found the way to raise money in time for that family and we'd never had patched things up between us again.

Tonight, Stefania and friends insisted on paying for mine and Joe's meals. They all chipped in together and nobody would listen to us arguing over it. There was one thing we were able to do though, and that was to leave a good tip for the patient and hard-working waitress.

I began to feel myself slide into a bit of a downer. I'd enjoyed finally spending some time with Stefania even though it was our last night in Siena. She was a person who stood-up for her friends and beliefs and I respected her for that. When we'd said thank you and goodbye to everyone in the restaurant, Stefania walked outside with us for a moment.

'You can stay, you don have to go yet,' she said.

'I think I have a bit of a headache coming, so it will be best if I went to bed.'

I gave a little squeeze to Joe's hand to try to let him secretly know I didn't want him trying to persuade me to stay. The truth was, I knew I wasn't going to feel very sociable sooner or later. I was already feeling sad about saying goodbye and now that time was looming, and I also had the trauma of meeting Mum and Dad tomorrow and to face whatever the consequences were.

'Let's exchange telephone numbers, so we can speak when I'm back in England,' I said, 'do you use WhatsApp?'

'*Si certo*, we use WhatsApp here too.'

'And maybe one day you can come to stay with me,' I said.

'Cool,' Stefania said through a laugh. I think she'd heard me say that too many times.

In turns, me and Joe gave her a hug.

'*Ciao* Stef.'

We walked up the little hill leaving behind us the happy sounds of a busy trattoria and continued walking away silently arm in arm.

21

Farewell

I wouldn't know how to begin describing my feelings when I woke this morning at eight thirty. Today for me was going to be D-Day; not doughnut day, not dish of the day day, more like dismal day or disgraced day.

Me and Joe decided to stay in his room last night, but in hindsight it might've been better if we'd slept separately. You see, I'd left the trattoria on a bit of a downer having said goodbye to Stefania as well as knowing that our time in Siena was coming to an end with the final showdown at the hotel today, so I was finding it more and more difficult pulling myself out of the mood I was in.

Joe was trying his best to cheer me up love him, and all I did was push him away. He seemed too relaxed as if it didn't bother him what was ahead of me, and there I was fretting my socks off. He kept telling me that I wasn't to worry about it so much, that everything works out in the end and I told him, not with my Dad it didn't.

So last night we kissed goodnight and that was that. Except I drifted in and out of sleep again worrying so much about meeting Mum and Dad today and what type of punishment they'd dish out to me.

I couldn't decide if having my phone taken away would be worse than being grounded. Then I thought, what if they banned me from ever seeing Joe again if they'd assumed he'd been a bad influence on me. Anyway, they could think what they liked; Joe has been, I mean is, a special person to me and if the punishment was to be the latter, I'd still see him, no matter what it took.

This morning I hated myself for the strop I was in. I didn't think that poor Joe knew what to do or say in case he got a sharp answer, especially if it was to do with my parents.

'I'm sorry Joe, I can't seem to relax.'

'Don't worry, I know how it is.' No he didn't.

We needed to pack up our things so he could check out of his room and then I had to do the same at mine, and in between, we had to find out which bus we needed to take to be dropped off near Hotel Rosaria.

We thought we'd go to Piazza Gramsci near the gardens along our way, because that was where we'd seen Stefania and so many other people catch buses and it was closer although Joe had originally arrived near the train station.

'Can you make out anything from that?' I asked as we both tried to understand the printed urbano and extraurbano bus timetables fixed to the posts.

'Fraid not, I'm sorry, it's too confusing,' he said, 'I think we should go and find someone to help us.'

So off we went in search for the information. Luckily Joe was carrying a rucksack on his back and I had my bag which I thought must've been much easier than dragging a pull-along trolley over the old paths and cobbles like I'd seen loads of people trying to do.

It turned out that we had a couple of choices; either we could take a bus from Piazza Gramsci at two thirty this afternoon, or we could leave a bit later at four fifteen from the bus stops near the train station. My phone showed it was currently eleven twenty-five.

'Four fifteen,' I said without any hesitation and Joe grinned at me.

'I don't want to go yet.'

We went inside a tobacconists come-newsagents which sold bus tickets, and where Joe could practice speaking Italian in Siena just for a little bit longer requesting the two tickets we needed.

The last thing we had to do was to get my stuff and check out. I changed into my pretty swishy skirt even though it had a faded ice cream stain but it was the one I knew Mum particularly liked.

The man who owned the rooms said something to us when as usual, I knew that I looked pretty vacant. Joe appeared to be quite taken aback with what was said and I think he asked the man to repeat it before turning to me to explain whilst the man went off somewhere. I wondered what the problem was.

'He said that he saw us on TV and read the newspaper this morning, which he's just gone to get from the other room, and saying that he's going to donate what you're paying him for your stay into the bank for that family.'

'Cor,' I said.

The man returned holding the newspaper and opened it at page five. There we were, me, Joe and Stefania with the family in their home and the article written by the journalist. The photo was quite nice even though it was plain to see that little Nevena had backed herself right up against her Mum.

I asked Joe to really thank him and to say that the next time we're in Siena, we'd stay with him again and that I was sorry if he'd heard me being sick the other night. He'd told Joe that apparently he'd thought it was someone outside. I should've kept my mouth shut.

I found the two hundred and seventy euros I'd kept separate from the tiny amount I had remaining, and handed it to him hoping that he was honestly going to pay it into the bank for that family. We shook hands and said *arriverderci* then stepped out into the hot air. With that done, I was another step closer to seeing my happy parents. Not.

'Come on,' Joe said, 'I'm needing a roll and a coke, how 'bout you?'

I didn't really have much of an appetite because those giant butterflies were coming back.

'Could murder a cold beer,' I said putting on a silly *please* pout with my lips, for which he tutted and raised his eyes in a way to tease me.

'Yeah, grand idea,' he said, 'pizza takeaway restaurants usually have beer in fridges, so what say you about going to that Vico's place you told me about. Do you remember where it is?'

'Not exactly, we could spend too long looking for it.'

I knew that it wasn't far away but I didn't really want to go there and be reminded of that night when he was shouting things at me down the street and anyway, who's to say if he'd changed his point of view about us since we shook hands.

'You're right,' he said, 'we can't risk missing the bus.'

'No.'

I wanted to say a sort of *arrivederci* to the Piazza del Campo and so along the way we bought ourselves a couple of cokes (because in the end I thought it best if I didn't turn up at the hotel smelling of alcohol) and some of that nice focaccia bread stuffed with tuna and tomato from a sandwich shop.

I also wanted to sit right in the middle of the square for the last time and consequently dragged Joe to a spot I'd decided had to be the centre.

'Didn't you just love it here, Joe?' I asked after finishing a mouthful of focaccia.

'Do you mean here-here or here Tuscany,' he replied.

'Here, Siena.'

Joe was just about to answer when I chipped in.

'Forgetting Vico's fist.'

'Well, it's been eventful, I'll give you that, but apart from one or two things that's happened, the atmosphere and grub has been great.'

'Anything else?' I said, 'I mean, is there anything else which sticks out in your mind, something you wouldn't forget?'

'Actually, yes.' Then he paused a while.

'Rubbing that lotion onto your skin amongst some of those things that happened to come up as a consequence.' He gave me a cheeky grin making me feel like being all naughty again.

'Umm, yes, that *was* super nice', I said, 'and a shame we've gone and checked out of our rooms.'

I really felt like climbing all over him at that moment but there were just too many people sitting close to us. We'd already been in the papers and I definitely didn't want to be in the Siena headlines for having sex in the city, and the newspapers printing something like, *Head shave couple disrespect Piazza del Campo and get arrested.* Imagine that.

'But *is there* anything else you want to add?' I'd been hoping there was something else he wanted to say.

'How about,' he said, 'meeting a very pretty stuck-up girl who ran away from her parents, but really, she is a kind and caring girl who loves fun.' I gave him a friendly thump. It wasn't that I was hoping to hear.

'And how about you,' he asked, 'what sticks out in your mind?'

'Oh, well, it's been an interesting few days,' I said, 'and I'm glad that you came to search for me.' *And I love you*, I thought.

What was missing was that neither of us mentioned about meeting up in Bristol on our return. I didn't want to bring it up, not yet, because I was worrying about finding out if it *really* was going to be just a holiday romance after all and leaving me feeling hurt. But I couldn't tell as to what he was really thinking. *No, come on I'm wrong* I said to myself, *he'll definitely want to see me when we get back, I'm just a born worrier.*

We finished our focaccia and the rest of the cold refreshing coke sitting close together taking in the atmosphere of that very historical and famous square. There was no traffic noise or pollution, just a hum from the hundreds of voices echoing around the buildings and the distant clinking sounds of cutlery on plates and teaspoons in coffee cups.

From where we were lying down, we could see the huge clock face on the tower showing that it was almost three o'clock which meant it was almost time to leave. We'd been lying there for ages with our heads resting on our stuff. Now and then we'd say what we thought a white and fluffy cloud resembled as it passed over above us. Sometimes our ideas were a bit too ridiculous and we'd end up getting the laughs. And other times, we'd stop and listen intently to people speaking near us and we'd make guesses as to what the languages were.

And so, it was a beautiful way to spend the last hour or so in that square until Joe had to pull me up onto my feet and convince me it was definitely time to leave otherwise we'd miss the bus and I'd be in more trouble. That got me moving.

Someone sitting in the opposite row of seats on the bus must've heard us speaking English and he was telling us we should've stamped our tickets in the machine at the front of the bus as we got on. He said that if the ticket inspector checked our tickets, we could've had a fine. Joe looked a bit surprised and told me that he didn't stamp his the other day.

I watched Joe wobble his way down the middle section of the bus to validate our tickets as the bus travelled along the hectic outer city roads of Siena. Better than a fine.

I was sitting in the window seat on the right hand side of the bus, so I was able to look at people or the shops and eventually, the countryside leaving Siena a long way behind. I didn't mind Joe chatting to the bloke because I wasn't in the mood for being talkative as I was trying to deal with my giant butterflies wondering about how it was going to be meeting Mum and Dad.

That moment was fast approaching, a lot of the people had already got off the bus including the bloke Joe had been passing the time with and so there were only a couple of other people remaining. It was a strange journey; I was recalling my journey of a few days ago when I was hitching a lift. I saw the big Palio poster still on the board and then the table where I sat and drank my coke I bought from the bar. Then not that long after, the bus started to slow down and it stopped just along from the turning to the hotel's gravel track. Those butterflies were so bad, I felt sick.

We climbed down the steps of the cool air-conditioned bus onto the side of the road and said *grazie* and *arrivederci* to the driver, who pressed a button making the doors swish shut before he pulled away leaving me and Joe all alone. I opened my bag and took out the two peaked hats we'd bought from a souvenir stand, one dark blue for Joe and the other black which was mine, and the words Siena University embroidered on the front. We put them on our heads.

'I really don't want to go,' I said.

'Come on beautiful, let's get it over with.' Joe held my hand whilst we walked along the track towards Hotel Rosaria with all its glory, which at that moment, I couldn't have cared less about.

The late afternoon sun was still really hot and I was sweating buckets. At that moment I'd liked to have been back in Siena with Joe sitting in some gardens and sipping something cool instead of walking up to the main entrance of that hotel.

'Can you go first Joe, please.'

'Course.'

He stepped into the entrance and the doors opened. There were two people working behind the reception who looked up at us as we approached them. We put our stuff down onto the marble floor.

'We'd like to know where mister and missus Wilmot are please,' asked Joe.

'I believe they are on the terrace,' the woman said. My heart was thudding. Why couldn't they have been out somewhere, for the day or the evening, I thought.

'Come on, you can do it.' Joe briefly lifted my cap and kissed me on my bald head.

I knew I really didn't have any choice and took a deep breath as we walked towards the glass doors with the swishy long white curtains that opened to the terrace. *Here we go then*, I said to myself.

There they were, my mum and dad were standing with their backs to the hotel building and looking out over the views of olive trees and grape vines. I wondered if they weren't looking forward to returning to Bristol as well; that they'd had a great time together and they were taking their last glimpses of the pretty surroundings just like we did in Siena. They looked lovely together, Dad, just a bit taller than Mum and I could see they'd caught a lot of sun. I was sure they didn't realise we were standing a short distance behind them.

I let Joe's hand go free as I walked slowly up to them, keeping my tattooed wrist facing inwards towards my body.

'Mum, Dad,' I said. My voice sounded nervous.

The moment I'd been dreading had finally come. They both turned round and threw me totally, when I saw them both reach out their arms to welcome me back. I rushed to them where they hugged me for quite a while before anyone said a word.

'I'm sorry,' I sniffed, 'truly I am.'

'You're a head strong girl, Caylin,' Dad said, 'but I have to say you've got guts.'

'Yes, maybe too much sometimes,' added Mum, 'but you're a compassionate and thoughtful being.'

'So, I'm not grounded?' I asked while keeping my tattoo firmly out of sight.

'Well, we'll speak about that when we're home, but firstly the deal is, we need to have a talk about taking risks,' Dad said. 'If it hadn't had been for Joe finding you and keeping us updated, the consequences could have been much different.' *Ah, so they knew a lot more than I'd thought and all that time I was dead scared, Joe had been giving them the latest, the rat.*

'Secondly,' Dad said, 'You'll be coming with me to the TA centre to learn a thing or two.'

Oh no, really? I thought. But it was heaps better than I'd been expecting. I looked to see if I could spot Joe somewhere, but he'd gone, I guessed he wanted to leave me with my parents to sort things out. Of course he had to find his parents, or shall we say, auntie and uncle.

In one day, all my emotions seemed to have been in turmoil, with the final occasion of the evening meal which was an end of tour farewell dinner attended by Nadia the tour representative.

Still wearing my black Siena University cap, I followed Mum and Dad out onto the terrace once again, keeping my eye open for Joe. It looked as though he hadn't arrived downstairs yet and I wished he'd hurry up as I couldn't wait to see him.

Mum and Dad found places for us to sit where we waited for others to arrive and all I could do was firmly fix my gaze on the open doors leading out to where we were. And when I saw him come outside with his aunt and uncle, I noticed he wasn't wearing his cap and that he wasn't worried about showing his shaved head. He seemed to have an air of pride about him and I just wanted to get up and run over to him and hug him.

I could see his eyes scanning the tables until they reached mine, when he gave me the most stunning smile. I grinned back at him and at the same time, pulled the cap off my head and put it away in my bag. I so much wanted him to come and sit near us, but the nearest seats had been taken and I had to watch Joe pull out a chair further down along the table. I knew I had to be patient and I also knew I really had to give my parents a bit of my time.

From where we were sitting, I could see how the relationship had changed between the stuck up woman in her heels and the well fed bloke; it was simple to tell they'd finally hit it off together and were evidently in love. I wondered if she'd actually managed to finish her article. Close to us was Nadia, who incidentally, still had her huge sunglasses perched on top of her head; she was chatting to the couple of older women.

As far as I could see, it looked like everyone from the tour was attending the meal except for the two younger women who'd won the money. Perhaps they'd found fun with the guys Mum had told me about and I hoped they wouldn't miss the coach back to the airport early tomorrow morning.

I tried my best to join in with the conversation around me, as well as having to respond to the inevitable questions about my days spent in Siena. It was difficult keeping my eyes away from Joe. I had to be patient.

Then two amazing things happened; the first was when a waitress came to the side of me just after we'd finished eating some grilled meats and passed me a folded white serviette; *from Joe* was written on the outside. Just for a tiny moment, I couldn't help wondering if it was going to be a goodbye note, something like a *It was great fun being with you in Siena, catch you in Bristol sometime*, type of note; after all, I didn't think he'd bargained for meeting someone quite like me.

I unfolded the white serviette immediately. The moment I saw what Joe had written, I caught my breath. He had drawn a type of Manga boy, with a shaved head. Next to it he'd written, *I love you*.

I felt dizzy with happiness and love. What a wonderful romantic gesture, and it annihilated all my worries about whether Joe and I would meet again in Bristol after the tour. I was already feeling thrilled about the prospect of being able to show Joe off to everyone back home. Then I realised I could feel Joe's eyes on me, waiting for me to look at him. When I did, I mouthed *I want to kiss you* and I gave him my best smile.

The other amazing thing, person in fact, was my dad. Yes, he'd been enjoying the wine, but I knew he was in full control of himself when during dessert, he stood up at the table and clinked his glass with a spoon to get everyone's attention. Then he cleared his throat before he began and I was flabbergasted.

'Most of us have witnessed what our daughter, Caylin, and her friend Joe have done for the family in Siena,' Dad said.

Pulling a *yikes* face I glanced quickly at Joe and back at Dad again.

'And although I have some issues regarding Caylin having disappeared alone to the city,' Dad added, 'I think we should congratulate Caylin on Joe on their courage and kindness in raising money for the family.'

There was a lot of cheering and clapping of hands, and I noticed that even others who were on a different tour to ours, were joining in. I was relieved to see Mum was clapping too.

'And Hotel Rosaria has offered to receive any donations at the reception, for example,' he gave a little cough, 'euros you may not want to take back to the UK, and they have promised to send the collection to the bank in Siena in favour of that family. Thank you very much.'

I was just so happy, after worrying for sooooo long over how Dad and Mum were going to react when I returned to the hotel.

When Dad sat back down again, I went to him and gave him a hug.

'That's *brilliant* Dad,' I said, '*you're* brilliant.'

THE END

ACKNOWLEDGEMENTS

I would like to thank James Essinger of The Conrad Press for being my mentor and coach enabling me to finally write my first novel (any mistakes remaining are entirely my own), and I must thank my supportive husband Derek for continuously encouraging me never to give up.